Inn of the Condemned

Jose Neptuno Martinez

Follow me on social media:
YouTube: www.youtube.com/@NeptunoMartinez
Instagram: @neptunomtz.escritor
Facebook.com/neptunomtz
TikTok: @neptuno.books
www.neptunomartinez.com

Cover design: Edgar Vega
Find him on Instagram: @grime_205
Book translation: Jose Neptuno Martinez
Original title: *La posada de los maldecidos (2022)*
Published by: Jose Neptuno Martinez
Book design: Jose Neptuno Martinez
Second edition

ISBN: 979-8-218-49798-9

For Yeimy, Sebastian and Aidan

With love for my parents: Minerva & José Luis

CHAPTER 1

They arrived at the place at the appointed time, as the security guard had recommended. According to him, it was the ideal time to go unnoticed. They would have the advantage of daylight since there was no electricity in the compound. Quarter to 10 on Monday morning: just as the rush-hour turmoil of bureaucrats, clerks, and others pouring into work at nearby places ended. The guard would discreetly open the entrance gate for them at that time. Close to the site, only the employees of the food stalls surrounding the building and some other street vendors would be around. The vendors were so used to seeing people coming and going that they didn't even pay attention to bystanders anymore—a point in their favor.

The security guard intended to justify their presence by claiming they were maintenance personnel. Three men in coveralls, carrying tools and backpacks like those used by campers, could easily pass as maintenance workers. However, when he noticed they didn't resemble the usual staff, he almost had a heart attack.

"What the heck, man! What's all that stuff you've got there?" the guard exclaimed, his eyes wide with shock.

"What are you planning to do? You're gonna get me in a whole lot of trouble! Vandalizing someone else's property is a crime, and I'll be the one who ends up paying for it! Remember when I said that this place might already be considered some kind of national monument or something? Weren't you supposed to be here for the same reason as everyone else? You know what, I think I've changed my mind," the guard said irritably, shaking his head. He was a good-natured-looking guy in his early sixties, but he seemed older. Maybe life had mistreated him. He held a position that, for many, was the last option since there were not many who liked to take such jobs. He wore the typical uniform provided by private security companies, which, far from impressing, caused pity. The poor pay did not justify free problems at all, but that was precisely the advantage point considered by the person who contacted him the day before to negotiate admission to the place.

"Relax. We are like the others, my friend. We are not going to destroy anything; on the contrary, we are going to improve many things," answered the one who appeared to be leading the group with a complacent smile. The day before, the guard had already shown a slight reluctance to be bribed when that person approached him. The main reason was that the owners—who, *by the way*, he didn't even know—had been very strict in their orders: prohibit access to marauders and adventure hunters and immediately report the presence of intruders to the police. Many had been taken to jail because people liked to get in and wreak havoc. The place already had a terrible reputation. Additionally, the looks of that guy had given him a bad feeling.

To break his sense of duty, the presumed leader quadrupled the amount he had offered up front. That worked, no surprise. The poor pay of the position was incentive enough to avoid being the hero of the day. He would gladly feign ignorance in the face of any questioning.

He imagined himself shrugging as he justified his actions to the bosses: *"They told me they were the maintenance crew; how was I supposed to know?"* He only asked them to avoid being seen in the courtyard corridors to prevent drawing the attention of the neighbors, whose houses were next to the property. They were known for being nosy and loved to concoct all sorts of wild stories. Several nearby government offices had a clear view of the interior, but that wouldn't be an issue since bureaucrats aren't interested in wasting time looking at rundown places; they prefer to pay attention to more important matters, like counting the minutes until the end of the workday.

"Aren't you afraid of ghosts, boss?" he asked as he opened the gate.

"The living are more to be feared than the dead" answered the group leader.

As they entered, the guard gave them one last piece of advice: "Don't forget to leave the tribute to the girl."

"Why don't you go to hell, *pal*," answered silently with clenched teeth and a wry expression.

CHAPTER 2

They couldn't waste time; they weren't there for a tourist visit, even though the place was worth it. Their objective was clear, and they knew what they were going for. The sooner they finished, the better. The daylight hours slipped away like fine sand in an hourglass. Even though they carried flashlights, the absence of natural light tempted darkness to become their worst enemy, especially when they had saddlebags to fill. They expected to finish that same day. There was no option; they couldn't leave the job halfway nor return the next day. It was risky. Much was at stake. The best thing was to take everything they could and disappear.

At first, they doubted the veracity of the information they received. Still, after finding themselves in the place and with the background they investigated, they were convinced. All the pieces fit together perfectly. Their expectations were high. They fantasized about what the future would hold for them from now on. They looked for a space at the main entrance to settle down and study the blueprints of the place. They had been supplemented with additional photographs, making the building familiar to them, almost like being at home. They just had to locate the starting point on the map. They settled at a dusty wooden table in the corner of the great hall and spread out the blueprints. The space was expansive, with large windows showcasing the overgrown grass of the lush gardens. This grand reception area could have once hosted royalty. Now, it was merely a sad reminder of what could have been—or perhaps what was, for a time. Despite the abandonment, it didn't feel like a gloomy place, contrary to what most people said about it. "*Ghosts, my ass, we've seen worse,*" thought one of them.

They took off their backpacks and put them aside, stretching their muscles. The tools they carried were heavy. A tall, corpulent individual, about six feet tall, with a stern face and sun-tanned skin, and another of medium height, slim build, aquiline nose, and the expression of a sectarian leader, began to examine the document, identifying places with his index finger. They watched and pointed to the surroundings.

"That's where it must be," said one of them. The third, a short, obese man with a mustache and bushy eyebrows, was distracted, looking at the cell phone, focusing on some photographs. His expression held a hint of lust.

"Still looking at pictures of that girl, huh, Filiberto?" the burly man said with mock exasperation.

"I fell in love with her. She's stunning. You have no idea how badly I've wanted to be with her since last time, Nacho. You two jerks interrupted me," Filiberto replied, shaking his head.

"There will be time to go back and say hello to her. I must admit that girl got me pretty *worked up*, if you know what I mean," Nacho, the burly one, said with a sarcastic grin.

"Hey! Hold on a second, you assholes. I'll be the first," Filiberto said, pointing a fiery finger at Nacho.

"Enough of this, will you? Stop the nonsense; we can't waste time on trivial things. Believe me, when we find what we came for, there won't be any need to go looking for that woman, so, concentrate!" ordered Ramon, the skinny guy leading the project.

"This is where we should go," he continued, pointing to the location.

"There is a false wall that will take us to the entrance of the main corridor. I don't think it will be a problem for us to break through. Where the walls seem to be the thickest, it's in this part. We must not forget this other place, which is the mysterious point, the one to which the crazy man in the story referred. We don't know what's there, but if we are lucky, maybe it'll turn out to be better than what we came for," Ramon said, with an ambitious expression and pointing to various parts of the blueprint. The other two nodded.

"Let's do it then."

The place was desolate. Not a single soul was to be seen. Considering the hour, intruders were unlikely to be at the site, so they could work freely. Furthermore, only they knew how to get to the specific point. If anyone else sniffed around, they'd walk past them.

They continued down a long corridor that led to a central courtyard, which bordered the vast rectangle of the great garden. They took the guard's advice and walked discreetly, almost sticking to the walls, because, as the guard warned them, one of the windows of a housing complex was almost in front of them. They could see the vast government building but realized it had many blind spots. For a moment, they were mesmerized by the place. Despite being in the middle of the big city, there was peace and tranquility like those which spring from a forest. Songs of birds and the air whistle caressing the grasses, plants, and trees could put anyone into a trance. Stone and quarry decorations added a special touch. It was inevitable not to stay to contemplate everything this place offered its visitors.

"What kind of place is this?" Nacho asked, looking from side to side. Filiberto focused his attention on one of the walls. "Isn't that...?"

"Enough already, you fools!" Ramon rebuked them.

"We're in a hurry; we can't waste time. The sooner we finish, the better. We're going to have time to sightsee places a thousand times better than this pigsty. So, walk."

They advanced. Ramon looked at the blueprints: "The entrance is here, up ahead. We must meet..." they paused.

"With a chapel?" Nacho asked.

All three wore the same shocked expression.

"And there, in the middle, standing is the crazy monk with his dog *spots*," Filiberto said sarcastically, pointing to some strange stone or quarry figures in a corner, guarding the entrance to what appeared to be a chapel. He was a pleading monk and a wolf in an attack stance. The three couldn't help but be amazed at such a collection of architectural whims.

"Let's go on," Ramon said, frowning.

They walked down to the final part of the corridor, down a couple of steps, and turned left, almost in a *U*. They left behind the central garden, the chapel, and the strange stone figures.

"It's here," Ramon said. "This is the entrance to the halls."

They were in front of a rusty metal gate. When they gave it a push to open it, it made a discreet screeching sound. A long, dark hallway appeared. At first glance, it resembled the corridor of an old hospital. Its length could be estimated at five hundred meters. Natural light managed to illuminate very little. At the end of the hall, as always, there was light. But they would not walk towards it but to another interior corridor; into the dark. Filiberto remained serious, motionless. Thoughtful.

"Oh... look at him. Already scared, you poor *chubby* boy," Nacho told Filiberto mockingly.

"And you're not? You sucker," he responded with a slap.

"We've been to worse places," Ramon insisted, "so let's go."

They entered the vast corridor and moved forward. Soon, the atmosphere was replaced by a sepulchral one. The silence was absolute. The temperature decreased with each step, caressing them. The place was gloomy. The abandonment was evident. They had to get the flashlights out.

The blueprints still guided Ramon: "A few more meters and we turn left."

"Whom the hell thought of building this place? These corridors are disconcerting; what is their fucking function?" Nacho grumbled.

"To hide exactly what we came to look for," Ramon replied, letting out a slight smile.

"We have arrived, gentlemen."

CHAPTER 3

They were in front of an entrance with a door that showed clear signs of being forced. It was almost hanging from the frame, just a step away from collapsing. They pushed it, and it didn't resist except for a slight groan from the rusty hinges. Now they were inside a room where darkness reigned.

"What is that over there in the corner?" Filiberto asked, his voice hurried, and his expression puzzled. All three directed their flashlights to the point. They froze at the sight of it. Amorphous figures, except for a round face with a maniacal smile, seemed to be watching them with wide eyes. They felt a chill that grew colder when they pointed their flashlights a few centimeters higher. What appeared to be a dress suspended in the air was present, but it was soon evident that it was hanging on the wall. The gloom began to play with their minds. Nacho took the initiative to approach, but reluctantly. He held tight to his flashlight as if the light emanating from it, was a protective shield.

"What is that?" he said dryly.

"It must be the girl's altar," Ramon answered with a smile that revealed a particular nervousness.

"It matches what we saw in the videos." Filiberto agreed.

A small wooden table was attached to the wall, with a makeshift board on top and a piece of plywood that gave it greater dimension. It was full of all kinds of chocolates and candies. In the center was a purple rubber ball with a face drawn. The look revealed a forced smile of fear. Or so it seemed, due to how the eyes and eyebrows were drawn. On the right were two small vases with some withered roses, and on the left was an old portrait of a little girl dressed in white. She wore a headband that resembled rabbit ears. Suddenly it seemed to them that the old dress, discolored and withered by the passage of time, hanging on the wall was the same one the girl in the photograph was wearing.

In the YouTube videos they had watched, they encountered all kinds of stories about what was said to be an improvised altar for a small, innocent girl who had disappeared in the corridors of the place. According to some accounts, government officials had used the compound in the past. Taking advantage of the large spaces, a nursery service was offered to employees. The girl was the daughter of one of the government employees, and during recess, when the children went out to play in the courtyards, she wandered away from her group and got lost in the corridors. It was said that after a few days, her lifeless body was found.

When the coroner analyzed her little body, they discovered the macabre finding that all her blood had been drained. Other versions claimed that the girl's body was never found, and she still wandered around the place, looking for her mother. Some charlatans claimed to have seen her running through the corridors, sometimes crying, others singing, and not a few playing pranks on visitors. She was the guardian and gatekeeper of that area of intricate passages. That is why an altar was set up in her memory, where candies and toys were left to ease her suffering and keep her happy. Everyone who passed by was obliged to pay tribute to her because, otherwise, it was said, the girl's curse would fall on the disrespectful one, and they would never leave the place.

"I'm amazed at how people love these bullshit stories, especially here in the southern part of the country. Very superstitious, these fucking *chilangos*," Filiberto said sarcastically while rummaging through the candies.

"These look good. I'm going to take a few for the road," he said, stuffing a handful into his coverall pocket and popping a marshmallow cookie into his mouth before tossing a pack of chocolates at Nacho.

"Don't be such an idiot! The girl's curse will come down on us," Nacho said with mock concern.

"Shut up, man!" Filiberto shot back, hurling the purple ball at him with force. Nacho shielded himself, and they both burst out laughing like a pair of goofy teenagers as the crazed-looking ball bounced wildly around the room.

"That's enough, you morons! What part of *we is* in a hurry haven't you understood?" Ramon said, raising his voice, frowning, and clenching his jaws. He shined the flashlight on both their faces in reprimand.

"Let's move on."

The location where they stood was an antechamber. To one side of the altar, a few meters away, there was another entrance, narrower and leading to another series of corridors. Darkness reigned inside. From time to time, glimmers of light could be seen through windows and doors in the distance, adjacent to the main corridor.

The entire area felt like a labyrinth, and without the blueprints in hand, they could easily get lost. Every so often, they felt a draft brushing against their faces, making the air feel cool, like the inside of a cave. They were grateful for their navy blue coveralls, which kept them warm. The coveralls reminded them of the ones Michael Myers wore. Instinctively, they each checked their cell phones to make sure they still had a signal.

"Do you want me to send a message to our friends?" Filiberto asked, addressing Ramon, who was a little thoughtful.

"Yes, write to them that we are a few meters away from

corroborating the authenticity of their story. It better be true. Otherwise, we will have to fulfill the promises we made to them."

"All right! Sent," replied Filiberto while looking at the photograph of the woman who aroused dark passions in him.

"I hope to see you soon, *hottie*," he whispered.

"We're about to reach the false wall that, according to this blueprint, is a meter and a half in this direction," Ramon said without taking his eyes off the document.

"Here it is!" he said with some emotion.

CHAPTER 4

A vast wall stretched to the end of the corridor. Gray, opaque, and graphite-like, it was decorated by humidity and the passage of time. They studied the place, touching the walls to find a hollow space. If they turned left, they would come across other chambers leading to unknown destinations. What was the real purpose of these facilities?

"Now I understand why the girl got lost," Nacho said, smirking.

They put their backpacks on the ground, opened them, and began taking out the tools. They set up a detachable work lamp and a couple of pickaxes and chisels. As they did, a sense of being in a zone of silence invaded them because the prevailing absence of noise was maddening and, to some extent, hallucinating. It felt as if they could hear their thoughts, as if someone were whispering behind their backs. Yet, the total absence of life was so significant that no rodent appeared, not even a miserable cockroach.

"Let's hurry up; I want to get out of here as soon as possible," Ramon said, indicating where they should start.

Nacho, the strongest, took the pickaxe and prepared to strike the first blow. If he hesitated, it was because he felt he was about to shatter the eerie silence enveloping them. He turned to see Ramon, who nodded. A loud knock echoed through the corridors like voices, though it lasted only a few seconds. They were surprised by the acoustics because, despite their efforts, the silence seemed to swallow everything. Better for them, as they gained confidence and began to hit the false wall with abandon. Dust filled the air. Stone, brick, and cement piled up at their feet. They made a big hole, revealing the secret entrance. Excitedly, they turned and focused their flashlights inside. It was impossible to distinguish anything; the blackness was absolute.

Nacho entered first, followed by Ramon.

"How about I wait here? To guard the entrance," Filiberto suggested, his voice trembling.

"Don't try to be a wise guy, you goddamn *fatso*," Nacho demanded, about to drag him in.

The interior was a narrow, elongated corridor whose end remained indistinguishable despite their efforts to illuminate it. The space was a perfect square, about eight feet high and wide. The ceiling bore arbitrary marks of humidity, time, and confinement, just like the first few meters of walls they could see. There were no signs of side entrances, openings, or windows. It looked like an endless, meaningless tunnel. The atmosphere was gloomy, funereal. It felt like being in a crypt.

The smell of confinement stood out above all. None of them considered themselves fearful, nor were they afraid of such scenarios; in fact, one could say they were used to them. Certain past activities had put them in worse situations, but the feeling that space aroused in them was disconcerting because they couldn't describe what it produced in them. Was it fear, anger, anxiety, envy, paranoia, or perhaps an amalgamation of all those feelings? Each one remained absent and abstracted for a few moments. *"Should we get out of this place at once?"* they thought. It was crazy—what the hell were they doing there? What madness had possessed them to venture into something that initially seemed like a hoax?

"Move forward", an inner voice seemed to tell them.

They took a few steps. The further they went into the tunnel, the colder and denser the atmosphere became. The sepulchral silence sometimes turned into tiny, almost imperceptible murmurs that seemed to come from the place itself. Ramon held the blueprints and asked Nacho to help illuminate them so he could study them more closely. Meanwhile, Filiberto felt an overwhelming need, almost an obsession, to look at the photos of the woman stored in his phone. His face expressed extreme lasciviousness.

"We'll see each other soon, my queen, we'll see each other soon... *Yes*," he whispered while typing something on his phone. He smiled. "I love you too, babe," he said, smiling at the response he imagined receiving.

Ramon and Nacho watched him from the corner of their eyes without understanding what he was babbling. Focused on studying the blueprints, they paid him little attention.

"The first point is about ten feet to our left. According to my calculations, the next one is about ten meters ahead on the right. Let's focus first on what we do know," Ramon explained.

"*Damnatio memoriae*," a whisper was heard.

"What did you say?" Ramon asked.

"I didn't say anything," Nacho replied.

They both turned to see Filiberto, still glued to his phone. The light from the device cast a maniacal expression on his face; he didn't seem like himself. Nacho couldn't help but think that Filiberto's expression resembled that of the rubber ball on the girl's altar. He smiled.

"Put down that damn phone and concentrate!" Ramon shouted, his voice creating a strange sound effect in the corridor as if hundreds of murmurs joined the reprimand. Filiberto turned with a grim expression and put the phone away.

"*Damnatio memoriae*," Ramon pondered. Where had he seen

that before? He unzipped his coverall and reached into an internal pocket of his jacket, pulling out a small felt bag. He emptied its contents into his palm. It was a relic of antiquity: two gold coins hinged together. Shining his flashlight on them, he saw the engraved word: *"Damnatio memoriae."* Nacho watched him without saying anything.

"Everything okay?"

"Yes. We better hurry."

They kept going, and as they did, they began to feel they weren't alone. Voices echoed hurriedly, like a small crowd. Muffled voices. It was bizarre, as they seemed to come from elsewhere. The sound effect was like a neighboring room's television at a low volume. The confusion heightened their alertness because that corridor had been sealed for years, possibly even decades, until they reopened it. No one should have been there. If someone had entered, it must have been from behind. Unless, at the end of the corridor, there was another entrance. But Ramon immediately discarded that idea when looking at the blueprints, realizing it was a dead end. The corridor ended at a thick wall forming part of the perimeter.

"It's the damn confinement playing tricks on us," Nacho growled, clenching his jaw.

As they continued toward the first point, they marveled at the wall's motley appearance. It seemed to have undergone constant repairs. Plaster joints, stucco, cement, and other materials decorated the surface. Ramon touched the walls. A chill washed over him; it felt like touching a corpse—an unsettling feeling. How strange. Why would a wall in a place meant for confinement be constantly repaired? What could cause its deterioration? Unless they were using it to hide something inside. That answer seemed logical. They felt both excitement and concern: what if what they were looking for had already been taken by someone else? They decided to pick up the pace.

"It's here; it's here!" Ramon yelled excitedly.

Filiberto and Nacho huddled together, illuminating the spot. They faced a wall, as expected, renovated. They were hopeful as soon as they saw the small initials engraved on the plaster: "*M.R. January 1982.*" The one who did that masonry work wanted to leave their signature for posterity.

CHAPTER 5

They placed the equipment on the ground, grabbed the pickaxes, and set up a couple of small work lamps with fold-out stands. They adjusted the brightness and angle of illumination. An insatiable ambition drove them. Nothing else in the world mattered at that moment, to the point that they ignored the eerie shadows forming around them due to the light. The attack on the wall was relentless. All three held the handles tightly and swung their pickaxes with force. As they did, a sick joy took over them; they laughed as they watched each other's faces. At times, they seemed to have gone mad.

Soon, they realized that breaking this part of the wall wasn't as easy as at the entrance. The wall resisted. Pieces of rubble fell, and small holes began to appear. The space filled with dust. As it dissipated, they took a break to catch their breath. They sweated, their faces twisted in revulsion as they discovered that the smell of confinement and humidity had been replaced by the stench of rot. They turned to each other, then covered their noses and frowned.

"What is that smell?" Ramon questioned.

"It must be Filiberto, who I'm sure didn't bathe," Nacho said sarcastically, with a touch of aggression.

"Get off my case, you jerk!" Filiberto snapped, gripping the pickaxe handle tightly to show he would defend his honor if necessary.

"What is wrong with you two? You behave like a couple of imbeciles. Let's focus, for God's sake!" Ramon exclaimed, just as something seemed to rush past him.

The three felt a small current of air.

"What was that?" Filiberto yelled.

They directed their bewildered gazes down the hall. They lunged at the backpacks, each grabbing a pistol. They cocked them and pointed in that direction.

"Don't shoot!" Nacho ordered. They stood still.

"Hey, who's there?" Nacho called out.

"I warn you, we are federal ministerial police agents, and we are armed. We will not hesitate to shoot at the slightest provocation. Whoever it is, you're trespassing. Leave immediately, and we won't take any action against you," Nacho announced, imagining it was the usual intruders.

There was no answer—just dead silence. The three remained pointing in the same direction.

"Most likely, it was a rat or a cat," Nacho suggested. They were silent for a few moments.

"It must have been that" Filiberto agreed, nodding.

They lowered their weapons, and just as they began to relax, a strange sound echoed in the distance. At first, it sounded like slow steps, but the pace soon quickened. The footsteps grew louder. Frozen, the three discreetly raised their weapons and stood on alert. The sound was intermittent, sometimes distant, then close. Their minds couldn't process what kind of noise it was until Nacho said, "Sounds like someone dribbling a ball."

They held their breath. The noise stopped.

"Someone is in the outside hallways. It must be the usual people who get in here to mess around. We need to hurry before they find the entrance. If anyone dares to come here, it will be their last mistake. What we're looking for is more important than anything else," Ramon said.

Nacho and Filiberto agreed.

"Let's hurry."

They took the pickaxes and resumed their attack. Gradually, the wall began to give way. Large chunks of brick and cement fell. The dust and light gave the scene a ghostly appearance. They managed to create a hole about a meter in diameter. They illuminated its dark interior. Their hearts pounded. They still couldn't see what they were looking for, but they were surprised to find that the interior space was a double wall with a narrow corridor about two feet wide. The front wall was built with stone, reminiscent of medieval dungeons. The foul smell of rot emanated from inside, mixed with humidity, making it almost unbearable. They donned face masks to make the situation more tolerable. Realizing that the hole would need to be enlarged for use as an entrance came to them quickly. Otherwise, extracting what they sought would be difficult, especially if it was as heavy as they had been told.

As they organized to continue the demolition, voices began to be heard in the distance. They were unintelligible but confirmed not to be impulsive noises or their imagination. They stood motionless, trying to make as little noise as possible. They signaled each other. Suddenly, the voices were replaced by deathly silence. Guns were holstered in the front pockets of their coveralls.

"Let's reorganize. There are people outside. Time is against us. Filiberto and I will finish opening the hole. Nacho, you're the strongest of us, so you need to go to the other point and start opening the wall. Let's use our time efficiently. According to the blueprint, it's about ten meters away. The specific point should be marked, just as it appears here," Ramon whispered.

Nacho glanced at the indicated point. His expression showed he didn't like the idea of going there, especially alone. Filiberto was about to laugh when Nacho's warning finger silenced him. Reluctantly, Nacho took one of the work lamps and the pickaxe.

Ramon and Filiberto began to strike the wall again. Nacho walked into the darkness of the corridor, shining the light from his flashlight. His steps were accompanied by the noise of his companions hitting the wall.

CHAPTER 6

Nacho was a corpulent and robust man, and he always used his size and strength to face any complicated situation. He dominated men and women alike, taking advantage of his stature and musculature. But as he walked down that hallway, he suddenly felt small and helpless. In the company of his companions, the desolation of that place was not so evident. But now, alone, he felt a biting cold, like hundreds of ants crawling across his skin. He refused to admit he was afraid, though it was inevitable, especially with the erratic shadows formed by the light's reflection. The effect was almost hallucinatory. He quickened his pace; he wanted to reach the point Ramon indicated as soon as possible, to finish once and for all with what he now began to consider a cursed quest. In the distance, he heard the frantic beating of a pick and chisel. He shone his light on the walls and found the repairs on that side even more erratic. The banging on the walls made him nervous; he was starting to feel annoyed. He wanted to yell at them to stop making so much noise. He needed to concentrate on finding the mark on the treasure map. He felt a light caress on his wide neck. He spun around in terror, feeling his chest about to explode.

"Who the hell is there? Is that you, Filiberto? Enough with your silly jokes!" he exclaimed in a shaky voice. He fumbled for his gun, which had fallen to the ground. He bent down to pick it up. He didn't see anyone, and it was evident it wasn't Filiberto because the blows to the wall continued incessantly.

"It's my conscience. I must concentrate," he thought, bringing both hands to his face while wiping the sweat from his forehead. He stood up and kept looking for the mark until he found it. He felt some relief. He adjusted the light to illuminate the wall and, once prepared, unleashed his fury against it. He became irrational, as he had been for much of his life. He wanted to smash that wall like it was an enemy.

The wall finally gave way. Ramon and Filiberto managed to make an entrance that resembled an archaic stone door. They were exhausted, breathing hard, and drenched in sweat. However, the desire to find what they sought continued to endow them with surprising energy. They leaned against the wall to drink some water. Their hands burned from the pick's handle. In the distance, they saw the light where Nacho was and heard the noise of his brutal blows. They smiled. Ramon stood up to enter the secret passageway. There was no time to lose. He asked Filiberto to wait at the entrance to be alert for any intruder. He walked through the narrow space and soon found several stacked bundles, which at first seemed to be body bags. "That must be it," he thought excitedly. He lunged at one of them.

They were large, thick cloth bags, resembling those used by athletes, covered in dust and cobwebs. He pushed one aside and shook it. Its weight was considerable. He took it with both hands and opened the zipper. His face transformed completely, his eyes bulging with joy that translated into a cry of emotion.

"What's happening?" Filiberto asked.

"We found them!"

Filiberto, leaning against the entrance, smiled. He took his cell phone and sent a text message. "We found the gold, my love. We're rich. See you soon." Just as he sent the message, he received a slap with a ball to the back of the head. The fact caught him entirely off guard.

"What in the…!" He turned bewildered. The purple ball took one last bounce and ended up at his feet. The maddened face watched him. He was paralyzed.

"Apart from the fact that you didn't leave a gift, you took my sweets," a voice of a girl complained.

Filiberto turned and was horrified to see the ghostly vision of a little girl in a white and bloody dress with a headband resembling rabbit ears. Her face expressed sadness, and her eyes, despite their blackness, were expressionless and absent. The strong impression left Filiberto paralyzed; his voice imprisoned, he could only release incomplete words, drowned out by the noise from Nacho's blows. Behind the girl, a shadow appeared, soon revealing a human silhouette. It was huge. In a guttural voice, he uttered a condemnation:

"Those who don't leave a tribute become a tribute."

Filiberto let out a howl: "Ramon!"

The girl and the shadow merged into a single amorphous mass of hundreds of miniature birds of prey whose flapping wings caused a deafening noise. With violence, the birds fell on Filiberto. His insane cry for help was swallowed up.

Still inside the corridor, Ramon listened to Filiberto tell him he would come in to help. He nodded without paying much attention, stunned by the contents of the bags. He heard Filiberto approach.

"Come see these *beauties*, Filiberto."

"How's it going, little friend? All in order?" a strange voice launched both questions.

When Ramon turned around, his heart pounded. He saw a man in a police uniform with a jacket, a black tie, and shoulder patches of faded yellow. The work lamp's light revealed the uniform was pale blue, but it looked dusty. He wore his police badge on the left side of his jacket, bearing the initials GDPT. The shadow from the police cap hid his face. Ramon trembled and discreetly moved his right hand close to his gun, ready to use it if necessary.

"Everything is in order, officer. As you might have noticed, we are maintenance personnel. The city government hired us to carry out some repairs because the walls are collapsing," he said, trying to hide his nervousness.

The policeman let out an intense laugh that echoed throughout the corridor. Ramon took advantage of the distraction, unholstered his pistol, and fired four shots that hit the policeman in the chest and face. The man didn't even flinch, as if he had shot at nothing. He took off his hat and, still laughing, pretended to wipe sweat from his forehead. Ramon saw a cadaverous face full of viciousness. A strange force immobilized him. His muscles tensed as if he were suffering from rigor mortis in life.

"You're going to have to accompany us to the police station, young man," the policeman said sarcastically. Two other uniformed men appeared behind him. They held something that seemed to be batons, but Ramon soon realized they were wooden sticks with pointed ends. They laughed maniacally as they played with them in their misshapen hands.

CHAPTER 7

Nacho stopped hitting the wall as soon as he heard the shots. He wasn't sure what had caused the noise. He was silent for a few moments, but since he no longer heard anything, he decided to continue his work. The wall began to give way, with huge cracks appearing. He felt they had used concrete to seal it off. A horrible scream emerged as he delivered the blow that opened the hole. Soon, stacked screams and pleas echoed in unison. The shock made him fall onto his back. As he lay on the floor, trying to sit up, he heard a girl laugh. He watched a purple ball roll toward him. He jumped to his feet like a frightened cat, only to find himself surrounded by four uniformed men in strange black robes. Yellow and red lines formed elaborate decorations on their chests. They wore pointed hoods with eyeholes, covering their faces. Despite his terror, he assumed a defensive and attack position. He was trained for it and had faced ambushes before. However, he quickly realized he had never encountered villains like these. A cadaverous hand grabbed him from behind. He maneuvered to free himself and, with agility, took that person or *thing* by the arm and threw him against the other three. They fell like rag dolls. With remarkable skill, like an old west gunslinger, he drew his pistol and unloaded the entire clip on them. To his shock, the hooded men vanished. Looking around, he called out to Ramon and Filiberto. There was no answer. Laughter and the distant voice of a girl filled the air.

"Nacho!" someone yelled.

He turned, searching for the source of the voice.

"Nacho! Over here!" the voice repeated. It sounded familiar.

"Ramon?" he asked with a frown.

"We're right here! Get us out!" Filiberto exclaimed.

He was stunned to realize the call came from the hole he had made in the wall.

"What the hell?" he muttered, plunged into extreme confusion. He walked over to the wall.

"Get us out of here, Nacho! Please!" both voices implored.

"But… but… what are you doing in there? How did you get in?"

"Nacho," called another dry, muffled voice from behind him.

He turned around to see the four hooded men standing before him. If there was one last memory in his mind, it was the feeling of his head smashing brutally against the wall. A fresh, bloody decoration had just been added to those damned walls.

The adrenaline coursing through Ramon's body gave him one last impulse to escape the spectral police officers. He took a handful of the contents of the cloth bag and threw it at them. They continued laughing. He sprinted down the narrow corridor and reached the gaping hole that now served as a door, but his progress was abruptly halted by a purple ball that tripped him. He fell forward, landing on his left arm with a sound like a branch snapping. The pain was excruciating. His arm had snapped in two, exposing a fracture. Wounded, Ramon began to crawl. The laughter of the police officers grew more distant, giving him a glimmer of hope.

Dizzy from the pain, he lacked the strength to stand. He leaned on his right arm to drag himself along, feeling something viscous. Looking up, he saw a terrifying sight: Filiberto's body stretched out in front of him, his lifeless face almost watching him with eyes bulging from their sockets. The last expression on his face was one of extreme terror. His robust body had been split in two from the waist. His viscera and entrails were scattered across the floor. A fetid odor hung in the air. The grotesque image locked Ramon's jaw. He couldn't breathe. Tears streamed from his eyes. He had finally known extreme fear. He noticed that Filiberto's mangled corpse held a cell phone. With great effort, he took it and called the first number that appeared:

"Help us! They are slaughtering us! Please...!"

It was the last thing he could say because something snatched the device from his hand while one of the police officers grabbed his feet and began to drag him. Ramon screamed, trying to hold on to the floor with his nails. Another officer turned him over. Ramon saw the same expression that the purple ball had stamped on the uniformed man's face. His expression was maniacal, smiling crookedly. A hard blow with the wooden stick landed on Ramon's face, and the lights went out.

CHAPTER 8

After what seemed like an eternity, Ramon began to wake. He felt weak and dazed, barely able to open his eyes. Not even in his worst hangovers had he felt this way. When he could finally focus, he saw something resembling a heavenly vault above him. Everything was sky blue. He could see landscapes, mountains, volcanoes, and lakes. He was lying on his back. The silence was no longer sepulchral—quite the opposite. There was peace and tranquility. The place was abundantly lit by the warm light of a few flickering candles.

"Where am I? Did I die?" he wondered.

Gradually, he regained consciousness and processed the images more clearly. He was under the dome of what appeared to be a church. There were fresco decorations and small oval windows of translucent marble along the entire circumference. From where he lay, he could see landscape paintings and scenes with various characters. Though his vision was cloudy, the candlelight gave the scenes a peculiar sense of movement as if they were alive. The dome had a second floor, and a wooden railing surrounded it. From the center of the vault hung an ornate lamp with intricate details. He felt watched and found the source of the gazes in the small statues of owls placed next to each of the oval windows. Impatient, he decided to stand but found it impossible since his feet and arms were tied to what seemed to be a ceremonial stone table, like a patient in a psychiatric hospital.

Pain shot through his being when he tried to move his left arm, reminding him of his fracture. He turned his head to both sides and noticed the structure of the place was circular, with large blocks of gray stone forming the surrounding wall. Gold-colored metal armrests were embedded in the walls along the entire circumference, suggesting the place was designed for people to sit.

"But… what the hell, where am I?" he muttered with concern.

He raised his head and saw a vertical rectangle with marble blocks veined in shades of brown. It was about two meters high and eighty centimeters wide. Inside the rectangle was a huge hollow cross that revealed a double wall. It was an altar with a seat in front of it.

"Help!" he screamed. "Please, someone help me!"

Murmurs and footsteps echoed.

"Who's there?" he asked nervously.

A girl's laugh echoed.

"Oh, Lord!" Ramon blurted out in a low voice.

He raised his head again, directing his gaze toward the altar. Behind the hollow cross, a silhouette moved from side to side, playing hide and seek. Intense yellow eyes, glowing as if electronic, became visible. He caught a glimpse of a crooked smile, like the one on that bloody purple ball that announced his doom. Panic seized Ramon. Just then, the four hooded men appeared, settling in pairs around the ceremonial table.

"Who are you? What do you want? Let me go! Please!" he begged.

The hooded men began to speak in a strange language while raising pointed daggers toward the dome. They sang a peculiar chant. During this, a uniformed policeman appeared at Ramon's feet. The light revealed his uniform resembled those of high-ranking officers, though somewhat outdated. His face was indecipherable and disconcerting, changing shape and expressions as if several people were disputing ownership of it. It managed to display one feature at a time: a look corrupted by arrogance and haughtiness.

Suddenly, the place was packed. Several men now occupied the seats along the circumference. Some wore high-ranking police uniforms like the man in front of Ramon, while others donned old-fashioned but exquisite suits, resembling corrupt politicians with cartoonish appearances. Their faces, though not cadaverous, expressed an absence of life. In the main seat before the altar sat a man with a light complexion, bald head, bushy eyebrows, and a small wide mouth. He wore an elegant suit. His face, despite its serenity, conveyed extreme cruelty and arrogance. His gaze pierced Ramon like poisoned pins.

Everything happened too quickly for Ramon to process. His brain was overwhelmed with emotions and thoughts. He didn't notice when cadaverous hands made several cuts along his femoral artery and wrists. The pain was excruciating. Compelled by some strange force, he turned to see the policeman holding a sharp broomstick.

"Oh, man, how much fun I'm going to have when I shove this stick up your ass and see how your little eyes pop out," the policeman said with a raucous laugh that echoed through the chapel.

The last thing Ramon felt was his life draining away, his blood flowing in a crimson spring. The blood ran through the small channels of a five-pointed star decorating the chapel floor, ending in a drainage system at the altar's base, emptying into the mouth of the underworld.

CHAPTER 9

Three months earlier.

Martin Robledo had been a tough guy all his life; he was not one to mess around. His look could be more severe than a punch. Over time, his character and temperament softened. Many said it was due to remorse. For what reason? Who knows. He kept many unspeakable things to himself, but some he revealed openly, and others were intuited. He was always very cryptic about his past.

Occasionally, he dropped a hint *here and there*. For those who got to know him in the last stage of his life, it was hard to believe that behind the face of that kind, aged man was someone who had once been a member of one of the most corrupt police forces in Mexico and perhaps in the country's recent history.

Of the few details known about his past, it was clear he began his police career in what could be considered the deformed sister of the Gestapo, the KGB, and the CIA—the infamous Federal Directorate of Security (FDS). This intelligence agency of the Mexican government, created during the 1940s to persecute and combat subversive and communist groups in Mexico, ended up being a solid and macabre espionage and political persecution apparatus against those who dared to oppose the so-called perfect dictatorship that ruled the country for several decades.

His passage through that agency was known only through an ID found in a box of memories. The blurred black-and-white photo suggested that in his prime, he was a good-looking man with a square jaw, thick hair, and 70s sideburns—the fashion of the times. More was known about his time in the General Directorate of Police and Traffic (GDPT) of the then Federal District government, today Mexico City. This agency was headed by the infamous Arturo *El Negro* Durazo, a Mexican official remembered for his outrageous and out-of-this-world corruption.

It was known that Martin Robledo met Durazo when he also belonged to the ranks of the Federal Security Directorate. When the former President of Mexico, López Portillo, appointed Durazo as top chief of the GDPT, he invited many of his old acquaintances and partners in crime to work with him, including Martin Robledo. During his time in the corrupt office under Durazo, Martin held various positions.

How many anecdotes and dirty secrets did Martin know about

Durazo? At one time, in a rather deluded way, he had considered Durazo a friend. How wrong he was. As soon as Durazo sat in the director's chair, and worse, when he was appointed division general by direct order of his friend, President López Portillo—much to the dismay of the Mexican army—he lost his humility and began to treat everyone dismissively. His arrogance and egomania knew no bounds. Not even the president behaved in such a manner, which said a lot.

Corruption in the GDPT had no limits; the abuse of office was blatant, and bribery and extortion reached legendary levels under Durazo. The capital's police officers became more feared than the criminals because *they were the criminals.*

One habit Martin acquired during his years in the GDPT and never fully shed was his fondness for good wines and expensive liquors. He recounted how some of the bribes required *under the table* when he was head of the driver's license office were paid in kind through the most expensive and delicate bottles. During family gatherings, after a few drinks, Martin told anecdotes of those glorious and disastrous years, mainly from 1976 to 1982, the six-year term of President López Portillo.

One of his favorite anecdotes was about the bacchanals organized by *El Negro* Durazo at his famous cabin at Kilometer 23.5 of the federal highway to Cuernavaca, a mountainous paradise near Mexico City. It was a lavish residence in the style of Swiss Alps chalets. These celebrations usually began on Friday, lasted through Sunday night, and were attended by nearly three hundred guests, including politicians, athletes, and artists from Mexican show business. Durazo used police helicopters to transport guests. There always came a point where Martin burst out laughing when he revealed that the waiters and cooks at these bizarre parties were none other than the GDPT police officers themselves.

"You're shitting me; I don't believe you! You are exaggerating!" some would say, astonished.

"Well, in that case, it's better that I don't tell you I even had to do construction work when *El Negro* built his cabin," he would point out, referring to the infamous anecdote of how Durazo used hundreds of police officers as masons for his construction projects.

Martin remembered with a certain contempt all the trouble they had to go through to move supplies to the Kilometer 23.5 cabin, including ingredients for the food and essential party equipment. It became a nightmare when they were told the top boss would have a party. The complaint wasn't so much about being distracted from their police duties but being forced to climb a kilometer of the hill on foot with all the essentials, as there was no road open to the public. A private one existed but was exclusively for *General* Durazo and his family. No roads or accesses were built for the public because, during the cabin's construction, Durazo's wife, as arrogant as her husband, ordered the architect not to build any roads, saying, "I don't want any roads here because where there's a road, everything fills with humans."

"I'm not making this stuff up, man," Martin would say, raising his eyebrows.

The demon Martin managed to shake off was his addiction to cocaine, a vice he acquired during his time in that disastrous government agency, somewhat by order of his superiors. To the disbelief of many, he said Durazo, and his high-ranking officers trafficked industrial amounts of cocaine, using police officers as dealers. The extra pounds that didn't make it to the market were distributed among the officers to make a little extra money. Everyone had to cooperate. That was an order from the brigade commanders.

"There was a lot of *speedball* left over you bastards! Take advantage of it; extra deal for the corporation!" was the order of Durazo's second-in-command, an obscure character known as *Pancho*, a most despicable guy. Since no one wanted to risk losing their job, much of the merchandise was acquired by the agents and other GDPT officials, who naturally became addicted. According to Martin, cynicism reached a surreal level where offering a *blow* was as normal as offering chewing gum or a cigarette.

Martin often told these anecdotes with a happy tone, inspired by a few glasses of wine. No one disputed he was a great storyteller.

"You should write a book, Martin," many told him.

"There's already one; you just can't get it, the criminal biography of Durazo, written by his Chief Assistant. The government ordered it to be taken out of circulation."

Martin always abruptly stopped his stories when he seemed to remember something that caused him significant discomfort; his face immediately gave him away, and his eyes took on a bizarre expression as if he harbored a mixture of hatred and regret. He seemed to enter a trance.

"Keep telling the story, Martin," they would ask.

He would look at everyone as if waking from a bad dream, become infuriated, and revert to the ironclad agent of the Federal Security Directorate.

"The story is over, you bastards!"

This was what Braulio Robledo told Fabiola Segovia, his girlfriend, as they headed to the funeral home where the body of the man who in life bore the name of Martin Robledo lay. He had died on Three Kings Day, at the beginning of the year.

His death was not unexpected. In his final years, he had an awful time due to colon cancer that tortured him. After so many chemotherapies, he looked like the mummy of Ramses II.

Of that strong and gallant man in his prime, only a few blurry photos from the eighties, where he appeared in his GDPT police uniform, remained.

CHAPTER 10

Braulio drifted through the streets of Chihuahua City, lost in thought. January had always been a month he despised, primarily for the chill it brought to every aspect of life. Undeniably the harshest stretch of winter. Even as a child, this month evoked a somber mood in him, and now, with his uncle Martin's passing, the gloom deepened. That cold morning, with a misty sky covered in clouds like chalk smudged on a blackboard, only intensified his sorrow.

"You're awfully quiet, babe. Cheer up a little," Fabiola said, gently caressing his cheek.

"I'll miss him. I'll miss his stories and our long debates about politics and whatever else. He was the last of a dying breed."

"You loved him a lot, didn't you?"

Braulio nodded.

"He was a remarkable man. All his experience, both good and bad, distilled into the best advice. I think, in a way, he saw me as a son and tried to make up for the father he wasn't to his own."

"I wish I'd known him better," Fabiola remarked.

Braulio and Fabiola had only been dating for a short time. He was an industrial engineer, and she, a lawyer. They met last summer when Fabiola's firm handled a legal case for Braulio's company. As the case required documents and information from Braulio's department, they began working together. They clicked immediately, and one thing led to another. She was five years younger, and according to Martin, they made a lovely couple. Fabiola met him just once, exchanging only a few words.

"You've got good taste, mijo," Martin had said, winking at him. *"The way she treats you tells me she's a good woman."*

Braulio took it as a good sign, given it came from someone quite knowledgeable about women. And he was right—Fabiola was beautiful, not just in appearance. She dressed impeccably, her attire perfectly complementing her delicate features, like her small mouth and long brown hair.

Braulio, with his rugged demeanor, was the opposite. Once an avid gym-goer, he had abandoned the habit due to work pressures. Taller than her, his square features lent him a certain gentlemanly air. He had that slightly disheveled look engineers are known for—jeans, sneakers, T-shirts, or plaid shirts. Their contrast suited them well.

"How did he end up in Chihuahua?" Fabiola asked.

Martin Robledo was Braulio's father Gustavo's brother. He moved to Chihuahua after the 1985 earthquake that devastated Mexico City. Like many from the capital, he lost his apartment and most of his possessions in the disaster. Martin's father, Don Gustavo, had emigrated from what was then the Federal District (Mexico City) after finishing his studies in the seventies. He wandered through various parts of the country until he took a liking to Chihuahua, where he settled and raised his family. Braulio was the middle child, with an older brother and a younger sister.

Before arriving in Chihuahua, Martin went through a cascade of troubles. In 1982, when President López Portillo's term ended, the country faced a massive devaluation and a severe economic crisis, mainly due to the outgoing government's poor decisions and corruption. The new president distanced himself from such a corrupt administration and launched a crusade known as "moral renewal." As expected, one of the most corrupt figures was *El Negro* Durazo, who fled the country before his imminent arrest. His corrupt regime in the GDPT crumbled, leading to a purge throughout the corporation. As usual, the low-level officials bore the brunt, including Martin Robledo.

At the end of the term, he was serving as the head of the Department of Banking and Industrial Police. With prying eyes on him, he fled to Los Angeles, California, for a year to avoid prison. Some whispered that the real reason for his escape was a failed assassination attempt. *Paranoid delusions from his cocaine addiction*, others claimed.

When the dust settled, he returned to Mexico City, married, and had a son. He worked as a private investigator for a while. By 1984, his life was in shambles: battling addictions, a failing marriage, and financial ruin. His legal troubles were numerous, including a brief stint in jail for breaking into public buildings. He quickly resolved the legal issue, thanks to a stroke of luck—a former GDPT colleague presided as the judge in his criminal case. Just as things began to stabilize, the 1985 earthquake struck, delivering the final blow to his finances. That's when Don Gustavo offered him support, allowing him to move to Chihuahua. He managed to kick his cocaine habit, found stable work, and remarried.

"What happened to the son from his first marriage?" Fabiola inquired.

"He always had a strained relationship with him. His issues and lifestyle drove a wedge between him and his family. The distance didn't help. Martin, who shares his father's name, stayed with his mother in Mexico City. They lost touch. Later, he tried to reconcile, but it might have been too late. I think my cousin held a deep-seated grudge against his father. Among the many things that haunted my uncle, which he never talked to us about, was his troubled relationship with my cousin."

"Do you keep in touch with him?"

"Not much. Occasionally, we'll like each other's posts on Facebook—that's about it. He's a tough guy," Braulio said, shrugging.

"Is he your age?"

"He's four years older."

There were few people at the *Rest of Eden* funeral home, located in one of the city's oldest neighborhoods, which made the atmosphere even more dense and sepulchral. That Tuesday was bleak. The biting cold didn't help. Martin had instructed his family not to bother with a burial ceremony or any other rituals when he died: "*What's the point? No prayer can change my course to hell. Straight to the grave, and that's it.*"

Leonor, his second wife, refused. "That's not Christian," she had insisted.

Braulio and Fabiola held hands as they entered the funeral home, walking through the corridors until they found the chapel. A small black plaque with white letters beside the entrance read: "Martin Robledo, 75 years old. Departed from this world on January 6, 2021."

Inside, pews lined the room, and the coffin lay at the far end. Braulio took a deep breath at the sight of it, his eyes welling up. Leonor sat in the front row, flanked by Braulio's parents. His older siblings, Rodrigo and Lety, sat a row behind them. Further back, three unfamiliar faces.

"You made it just in time; the rosary is about to start," his mother, Doña Martha, whispered when she saw him.

Braulio greeted his relatives with a nod and approached his aunt: "I'm so sorry, Aunt," he said, hugging her tightly. He had to stoop a little, as she was quite short. She was nearly fifteen years younger than Martin. Some of their acquaintances used to tease him about *robbing the cradle*.

"Oh dear, I'm going to miss him so much. Even if he was so grumpy and foul-mouthed, he was a good man deep down," she cried, her tears soaking Braulio's face.

Braulio approached the coffin. The man with a thousand stories lay behind the glass. At last, he seemed to be sleeping, for insomnia had been his constant companion. Despite his efforts, tears flowed down Braulio's cheeks. Fabiola moved closer, offering comfort. They spent a couple of hours at the funeral home, drinking bland coffee from foam cups and nibbling on stale cookies, sitting in worn armchairs, talking about everything and nothing.

Just as they were about to leave, Aunt Leonor approached Braulio and, with some discretion, said:

"*Mijo*, when you have a moment, please come by the house. I have something your uncle left for you. He gave me strict instructions to give it to you as soon as he passed."

Braulio was taken aback. What could his uncle have left him? He was caught off guard.

"He left something for me? What is it, Aunt?" he asked, curious.

"Oh, don't ask me, *mijo*. I only know it's a sealed box. He warned me not to even think of opening it or else he'd come back to haunt me, pulling me by the feet at night," she said with a small laugh that barely softened her sadness.

CHAPTER 11

It wasn't until Thursday afternoon that Braulio accompanied his aunt, Leonor Ortega—Martin's widow—to collect what could be considered his uncle's inheritance. He arrived at her home in a small suburb north of the city. His aunt welcomed him warmly, dressed in black. Being devoutly Catholic, she mentioned she would be in mourning for at least a month and cordially invited him to join the *novena*.

Braulio deftly managed to excuse himself.

"Here, have a cup of coffee to warm you up, *mijo*." Leonor also offered some cookies, lovingly baked.

They shared some anecdotes, drifting into melancholy. Braulio felt a twinge of pity for his aunt, left alone, plain and simple. They had not had children—apparently, not by choice, but due to some impossibility on one of their parts, or so the rumors went.

"I won't take more of your time, *mijo*; we've already chatted long enough. You must have many things to do," she said, somewhat embarrassed.

"Please wait a moment; I'll get what your uncle left you."

Braulio nodded.

It was only seven in the evening, but with winter's early nightfall, it felt much later. While he waited, Braulio wandered around the living room, glancing at family portraits—Martin and Leonor as newlyweds, vacations on some beach, and other settings. He picked up a photo where Martin appeared very young, likely an institutional photo. He was posed frontally, a serious expression with a penetrating gaze, dressed in a uniform. It was from his time at the GDPT during Durazo's reign.

"Here's what your uncle left you. He was very particular about it and insisted it be delivered directly to your hands. It's all yours." She handed it over with a hint of theatricality. The package was somewhat heavy, a box made of hard material, about the size of a shoebox, tightly wrapped with a label that read: "Recipient: Braulio Robledo."

Braulio was intrigued.

"Don't forget to tell me what *secret* was so jealously guarded," she said with a wink. He smiled.

"Thank you so much, aunt. Please, don't hesitate to call me if you need anything."

"Thank you, *mijo*," she said, giving him a big hug.

Braulio decided to go straight to his apartment. As he drove down one of the city's largest avenues, he put his phone on speaker and called Fabiola. He apologized for not being able to see her that night, citing exhaustion from work and still feeling a bit overwhelmed by his uncle's death. He preferred to be alone, he explained. Something inside him insisted that no one else should be present when he opened the package his uncle had left him.

"It affected me a bit to be in his house, to see my aunt and all the memories," he told Fabiola.

"What did your uncle leave you?"

"I don't know yet. It's a box. Could be some photographs or other personal mementos, I imagine," Braulio replied, downplaying the significance.

"I'll see you tomorrow, okay?"

"I love you; I hope you get a good rest."

He hurried into his apartment, tossing his jacket on the table before collapsing on the couch. The intrigue of the box's contents was too much to bear. He tore off the wrapping desperately—several layers in total—ending up ripping it apart like a child unwrapping a Christmas present. *"Typical of my uncle, always paranoid"*, he thought.

At last, it was revealed. A wooden box, possibly oak, with intricate designs and engravings. It seemed to be finely crafted, likely meant to hold something valuable—perhaps a bottle. He paused for a moment, thinking of his uncle wistfully, his heart pounding. He took a deep breath before opening it. He lifted the small latch that secured the box and slowly opened it, examining the contents with a frown. There were several items inside.

The first was a folded document, resembling an old road map. He unfolded it to find a blueprint of a building, containing several sheets with annotations and notes. Was it one of his uncle's properties? Unlikely. The building was large, far too grand for Martin, who would have sold it to spend his final years in luxury. He dismissed the idea and set the blueprint aside to continue inspecting the box's contents.

Next, he found an envelope containing old photographs, some in color, others in black and white, from Martin's time at the GDPT in the late 1970s and early 1980s. In the photos, Martin was seen with several individuals whose corruption was palpable even through the images. It pained Braulio to include his uncle in that assumption. Another photo showed Martin standing beside a tall, handsome man with square features and slicked-back hair. Both were dressed in suits, with Martin smiling.

Flipping the photo over, he read a handwritten note describing the unknown man: "With my good friend José González, Chief Assistant to General Durazo. The year 1980." Another photograph showed Martin receiving an award from General Durazo. The reason? Braulio had no idea. *El Negro*

Durazo's arrogance was evident, even in photographs. Martin appeared serious. *"Perhaps this was after Negro had fallen from my uncle's favor for being so arrogant"*, Braulio thought.

One black-and-white photograph was particularly unsettling. It depicted two well-dressed men who seemed important— perhaps politicians. Despite their distinguished appearance, their expressions were grim, almost macabre. One exuded arrogance and hatred, while the other, a thin, bald man with bushy eyebrows and a small mouth, looked sinister. The following photographs showed an old, abandoned building. Braulio discarded them quickly to continue investigating the box.

The next item surprised him even more—a USB flash drive with a simple, Chinese-made design. He turned it over several times, as if doing so might reveal its contents. He couldn't help but think that perhaps when his uncle assembled the contents of the box, he had already begun to lose his mind—delusions of a dying man.

There was also a small, worn book titled *The Blackest of Negro Durazo: Durazo's Criminal Biography*, Written by his Chief Assistant. The cover featured a photograph of three men in caps and gowns, with Durazo in the middle. The back cover read: "The complaint all of Mexico was waiting for!" alongside the author's photograph, a man Braulio recognized from one of the earlier photos with his uncle. He flipped through the pages and found a dedication: "With appreciation for a great friend, Martin

Robledo," signed by José González G. 1983.

"Why did my uncle leave me these things?" Braulio wondered, puzzled.

Only two items remained. One was a small black felt bag, heavy, with a circular object inside. He opened it to find two large coins—Mexican gold centennials, hinged together. The centennial is a coin minted in 1921 to commemorate the first centenary of Mexico's Independence. Minting ceased in 1931 and resumed in 1943 due to high demand for gold coins. The majestic angel of victory was depicted on the coins, holding a crown of olives in her right hand and broken chains in her left, with the legend "Fifty pesos" and "37.5 Gr. Pure Gold" on either side. He examined them closely; it resembled a massive locket. Venturing to open it, he discovered a series of engravings on the obverse, where the national coat of arms had been. The entire text was not legible, as it was clear someone had tried to alter the original engraving, replacing it with a new legend: *DAMNATIO MEMORIAE.*

Braulio was bewildered. The phrase meant nothing to him. In smaller letters, at the bottom, tracing the outline of the coin, the final part of the original dedication could be read: "... with respect, from your friend General A.D." Without a doubt, it was an ostentatious and ghastly gift for someone important. Bribes were the first thing that came to mind.

The last item was a letter. He hastened to open it, hoping to find an explanation for this strange inheritance. He took the document from the envelope, unfolded it, and began to read. His confusion only deepened. It was in his uncle's handwriting, full of spelling errors: "Dear Braulio, nephew. I was always terrible at writing, so I recorded a video instead. You'll find it on the memory stick I left you. Watch it; I'll explain everything. It's vital that you know certain things and free me from the hell that haunts me."

CHAPTER 12

Braulio's apartment was modest: one bedroom, one full bathroom, and a kitchenette. It had everything necessary for a thirty-four-year-old single man. The rent was affordable. Located in the traditional San Felipe neighborhood, a middle-class area of the city that had started to age until recent renovations of houses, shops, and apartment complexes, like the one where Braulio lived, began to rejuvenate it. Braulio had nearly married his previous girlfriend, with whom he had been in a relationship for almost five years. They decided to end things after realizing they had grown cold and distant. She traveled often, and he was consumed by work. Mutual infidelities also contributed to their separation. His mother, Doña Martha, and his sister, Lety, were unjustifiably anxious about his single status:

"Braulio, you're going to miss the train; all your friends are already married. Do you want to be alone for the rest of your life?" they constantly told him.

He just listened and gave them the *"yeah, yeah"* treatment. He had learned to take things slowly. After graduating as an industrial engineer, he faced the harsh reality of unemployment that haunts recent graduates until he finally secured a job in a tech factory where he worked like a slave for miserable pay. Things had slightly improved; he was about to complete six months in a better position, although the pay was still inadequate for his qualifications. *"I must not back down. This is just a phase,"* he reassured himself. His family was plain and simple middle class. They never indulged in luxuries, but they always lived comfortably. One of the most valuable lessons Don Gustavo, his father, had taught him was the art of patience and overcoming hopelessness.

Braulio took his laptop and placed it on the small dining room table. He quickly inserted the USB and navigated through the folder until he found the contents. There was only one video file titled *Posada*. Braulio was intrigued. The name meant nothing to him. He double-clicked to open the video. A small window appeared and then expanded to full screen. Martin's image filled the screen as he clumsily tried to position the camera. It seemed he had recorded it with his cell phone. The video was shaky. He muttered some curses under his breath.

Finally, the camera was steady. After stepping back and settling into a chair, Martin's withered face came into focus.

He looked at the camera.

"Is the red light on?" he asked softly.

Braulio recognized the dining room where the recording had taken place—it was the same room he had been in just a few hours earlier. A deep sadness filled his soul at seeing him still alive. He wore a plaid shirt and blue jeans that seemed too big for his thin frame. Braulio wondered if this recording was the last act of Martin Robledo's life.

"My dear Braulio, I ask for your understanding regarding the conditions under which I am recording this video and the reasons I will reveal here. I didn't dare to tell you this in person," he said, clearing his throat and taking a sip of water.

"Believe me, I always intended to, but I never found the courage, the way, or the right moment. It was as if something was holding me back. Guilt, remorse—perhaps I didn't want what I am about to reveal to you to become a burden or even a curse. Because, in a way, it has been that for me. It has haunted, tormented, and eaten away at me. Maybe it's what caused this damn disease that's killing me." He frowned and lowered his head. Braulio watched intently.

"I know for certain that I don't want to take this secret to the grave because I'm sure it would be my eternal curse. I know I have reserved a space in hell, but I'm certain I must lighten my load, atone for one of my many sins, and, most importantly, bring about good and justice for many." He paused to take a deep breath.

"No one else knows what I am about to reveal to you; at least, I hope so. Some of those who might have known are already paying their dues in hell. I would have liked to tell my son, Martin, but that's impossible because I ruined my relationship with him. Imagine springing this on him. His resentment could have turned into hatred towards me. Just the thought torments me," he said, shaking his head.

"With you, it's different, Braulio. As you know, I was always gruff, very inexpressive, but that doesn't mean I don't regret not telling you this face-to-face," he said, pressing his lips together and raising his hand to his forehead.

"I've always seen you as a son. My love for you is deep. I'm very proud of the man you've become; I admire your integrity and maturity." As he said this, a gleam lit up his face. Braulio was disarmed, and the tears streaming down his face forced him to blow his nose.

"That's why I know the secret I am about to reveal to you, in your hands, will not only benefit the family greatly but also bring justice to those who were wronged." He paused to drink more water from a bottle.

Braulio didn't take his eyes off the laptop as a thousand questions swirled in his mind. What could this secret be that his uncle had guarded so carefully? Why did he speak of justice for the wronged?

"Here goes, I won't drag this out any longer. Please pay close attention to what I'm about to tell you... Have you ever heard of the *Posada del Sol* hotel?" He paused briefly. Braulio had never heard that name.

"Most likely not, and it's better that you hadn't. But there's no other way. I don't have time to tell you the whole backstory. I'll only let you know what you need to know. The first thing I must tell you is that it's a cursed and *condemned* place where unspeakable atrocities were committed." Martin's face showed deep sorrow. He was silent for a few moments.

"Forgive me for being blunt, but that's how I've always been, and I don't like beating around the bush. The *Posada del Sol* is an old hotel that, much like its owner, fell into disgrace. Its construction has always been shrouded in mystery, and the stories surrounding it are filled with esotericism, witchcraft, and the like. Those are fairy tales compared to what I know. It's a structure that now lies in ruins in the *Doctores* neighborhood in Mexico City. At one time, the building was acquired by the city government and used as offices until López Portillo's administration, when the infamous *Negro* Durazo was put in charge of the city's security," he said, rage flickering across his face.

"There's so much I could tell you, enough to fill a book," he smiled, "but I'm getting sidetracked. I must be as specific as possible. Time is against me. Listen carefully, Braulio. Two great treasures are hidden in the *Posada del Sol* that deserve and must be rescued from that damned place. I'll start with the first one, which, in a way, is the least important, as I later came to realize when I regained some moral clarity," he said, shaking his head as if chastising himself.

"Hidden in the secret corridors of the hotel are what I estimate to be about *seventeen thousand* Mexican gold centennials. Yes, you heard that right! Maybe more, maybe less, but there's a lot."

CHAPTER 13

Braulio rewound the video to listen to that part again: "... *seventeen thousand gold centennials...*" He paused and brought both hands to his mouth.

"Holy shit!" He stood still for a few moments, trying to digest the statement.

He resumed the video.

"How do I know? Simple: I hid them", Martin said, shrugging with a mischievous expression.

"At that time, I worked as one of those who managed Durazo's loot. In the last stage of *Negro's* reign of corruption, I was appointed head of the Banking and Industrial Police Directorate under the GDPT. How did I get there? I'll tell you soon enough. Like a mafia boss, *Negro* Durazo received truckloads of money from bribes, extortion, payments for political favors, and embezzlement, among many other outrages he committed, thanks to his absolute power. The man refused to accept Mexican pesos or checks. He demanded that everything be given to him in gold or US dollars. His orders were indisputable. More than once, I witnessed how *Negro* ruthlessly punished those who dared to contradict him by paying tribute in Mexican pesos. Every fortnight, he received several suitcases full of dollars and centennials. The loot was always transferred to a secure location where only Durazo, his chief assistant, and a third person went. This last person helped carry the heavy suitcases and acted as a driver. *El Negro* frequently replaced that third person to avoid temptations and leaks of information because, in the end, he no longer trusted even his own shadow. It was only natural because the corporation became infested with the worst human scum. The driver received a stern warning—nothing more than a severe threat—to keep his mouth shut. At a certain point, *Negro* Durazo asked his chief assistant to find an exceptionally trustworthy person to fill *the position* permanently. The previous poor devil who had done such honorable work had talked too much during a drunken spree and received a beating that left him paralyzed. That's how those people were. Some real sons of bitches," Martin said, raising his eyebrows.

"At that time, I had an excellent relationship with the chief assistant because we had done some small jobs together. He trusted me completely. Not to mention that *El Negro* already knew who I was, even though he pretended otherwise. That piece of shit." He smiled sarcastically.

"They strategically assigned me as department head in the Banking and Industrial Police to avoid suspicion—not because I was the most qualified for the job." Martin laughed.

"Once the loot was delivered, the next step was to go to the headquarters of the then National Bank of Commerce. We drove to the basement, where the CEO was already waiting, along with other bank policemen, and we unloaded the suitcases from the trunk. *El Negro*, accompanied by the men and his chief assistant, took a private elevator. I was supposed to wait for them in the basement." Martin paused briefly, as if trying to organize his thoughts.

"If you remember your history lessons, you already know that the government of López Portillo ended disastrously. He left the country in chaos; a devastating devaluation swept through the economy like an overflowing river. The corruption of that administration, particularly Durazo's, was scandalous. His abuse of power was legendary. The new president had promised to carry out a cleanup as soon as he took office. Although they were from the same political party, the infamous PRI—the same *sons of bitches* as always, thieves and corrupt—they wanted to fool everyone and pretend to distance themselves from the corrupt. But in Durazo's case, it wasn't possible. He had crossed the line, and he knew it. And he also knew he couldn't go unpunished, so before finishing his term as head of the GDTP in late 1981, he prepared everything to flee the country and secure his loot. Time was against him. His corruption had been exposed, and everything got worse when his chief assistant, with whom he had ended in intense enmity, published a book publicly denouncing his boss's misdeeds. It's that little book I left you, along with the other things."

Braulio stared at the box; his surprise evident.

"The dollars were easily smuggled out of the country and deposited in tax havens. But the gold centennials? There were so many that it became a real problem. I never saw them all together, much less counted them. However, according to what Durazo's chief assistant disclosed to me, *El Negro Durazo* received a hundred gold centennials each month. Suitcases packed with them. Do the math. It was obvious that if those gold coins remained in the bank, the new government would *confiscate* them," he concluded, making air quotes with his fingers.

"By that time, he and his former chief assistant were bitter enemies, so he could no longer rely on him. One day in early 1982, Durazo's new right-hand man, a nefarious and arrogant figure who doesn't deserve to be named, replaced the former assistant and entrusted me with one final mission. I was to go to the bank's basement, where an armored truck awaited, guarded by several men. We loaded the truck with the gold centennials and headed to the *Posada del Sol* hotel, where we were to receive instructions for securing the treasure. Durazo probably thought that once the dust settled and he was cleared of the accusations, he could reclaim his wealth. The poor bastard miscalculated! He never returned because he fled the country, only to end up behind bars," he said, releasing a short laugh.

"It was a frigid day in early January 1982. You know the cold in Mexico City isn't like the one in Chihuahua, but that day, it was nearly freezing, especially in that cursed place. I remember it well. We hid the centennials in a secret spot within the *Posada*. It was there that I learned the true story of that damned place and the horrors that *Negro* Durazo and other fiends perpetrated over the years." The video captured Martin's discomfort as he lowered his head and ran his hands through his sparse hair. He took a deep breath and, with a shaky voice, continued narrating.

"We spent two days hiding the treasure. There were many suitcases and bags to unload, and we had to do some construction work. The place was creepy. I'd only heard rumors and legends about that ruin, never imagining how much truth lay behind them. Four of us handled the heavy lifting, which involved demolishing walls, digging, filling, pouring cement, and patching up. I was no stranger to this kind of work, as my companions and I had already worked as construction laborers when we built the mansion at kilometer 23.5. Four men in suits, with the appearance of thugs, expressionless faces, and bloodshot eyes, acted as foremen. They watched us like hawks, ensuring we didn't steal anything. *Hurry up, you bastards, and don't even think about pocketing any of those gold coins, or your bones will end up here*, they threatened us."

"I'd never seen them before. They resembled the corrupt detectives of that era, infamously known as *Federales*. I quickly realized they'd kill us without a second thought if we made a false move."

"Well..." he paused, clearing his throat.

"While digging and removing debris, we made a discovery. At first, I didn't think much of it, assuming I knew what it was. As a cop, I'd seen things like this before. But two of my colleagues quickly made it clear that I didn't have a damn clue. They explained the horrifying extent of what we found, something so brutal that even someone like me was shaken. They revealed that it was a site of nightmarish imprisonment. Hundreds of souls were condemned to a slow and agonizing death within those walls. Some of the remains we uncovered bore gruesome witness to that," he said, his voice breaking as tears welled up, his frail hands covering his face. He paused again to take a deep breath. Braulio leaned in; his brow furrowed in intrigue.

"Oh, *mijo*! I hate to burden you with this, but it must be done." He fell silent for a few seconds.

"But hey, hey! I must stay on track and hurry before your aunt gets here. She mustn't know what I'm telling you. When the time comes for you to act on this, you'll tell her what's necessary. I'm almost finished. Hang on a little longer."

"While we toiled with shovels and picks, those gorillas

brought us drugs, alcohol, and some burritos. *Come on, you junkies, take a hit so the load feels lighter*, they taunted us. The atmosphere in that place was so dark and surreal that we eagerly accepted their offer. We got *pretty damn high!*" Braulio managed a weak smile.

"As for me, I was glad to numb myself like that. Otherwise, I would've lost my sanity for the rest of my wretched life. At least this way, I could dismiss much of what I saw as hallucinations. There were moments when I thought we wouldn't make it out alive," he said, shaking his head.

"Braulio, listen carefully. What I'm about to ask may sound insane. I want you to go to the *Posada del Sol*, find the centennials, or rescue them from that cursed place, and use them for justice. I know what you're thinking, and that's why it's been so hard for me to reveal this to you. This represents a significant moral dilemma for a man of your integrity. You might think this is dirty money, tainted by corruption and cursed. But there's a deeper truth here. You can do good with it, including helping the family. Can you imagine what all that gold could do? It would change everyone's lives! You'd never have to worry about money again; my beloved Leonor would be free from her troubles, and her old age would be secure. And as for my son Martin and his mother, it could repair some of the damage I caused and give them in death what I couldn't in life." He raised his voice, slapping the table.

"Consider this: those centennials have no owner anymore.

Everyone who knew about them is dead, including *Negro* Durazo, who, as I learned, feared someone would steal them due to his greed. He didn't even tell his family where they were hidden. By the time he was released from prison, he was in such bad shape that I doubt he wanted to return to that dark place and stir up old demons. It would've unearthed a monstrous past. By now, the centennials must be nothing more than a rumor, an urban legend. I'm the last person alive who knows the secret, and now you know it too. I almost didn't live to tell it," he said, frowning slightly.

"Of course, the decision is entirely yours. I don't want you to feel obligated or think that I'm asking this as a dying man's wish that you must fulfill. I'll be honest: whatever you decide will be the right choice for me. Despite your youth, you're a wise man. I just wanted to lift this burden from my shoulders and give you an option to consider. And about that damned place, don't worry. For someone like you, the insidious effects of the *Posada del Sol* will be like foolish words falling on deaf ears."

CHAPTER 14

Braulio paused the video, resting his elbows on the table as he took a deep breath. It took a moment for his mind to process what Martin had just revealed. He placed his hand on his forehead, overwhelmed by a flood of thoughts. One pressing question gnawed at him, compelling him to continue the video in search of answers. It felt as though Martin had divined his thoughts in an esoteric act from beyond the grave.

"I know what you're wondering. In the box, I left a blueprint that serves as a map, along with some photographs of the Hotel *Posada del Sol*. I assume you've already seen them. I made precise notes on the exact location of the hideout. Follow them to the letter, and you'll have no trouble finding it. There are a series of false entrances and hidden corridors that no one knows about. Without the instructions and annotations I made, no one will ever locate it. You'll need tools and help—you can't do it alone. Although the *Posada del Sol* is currently closed to the public, it's become somewhat of an attraction for teenagers and ghost hunters. Many people circumvent security to explore. I've heard of some idiots who even act as guides for a few *pesos*. But none of those fools have found the hiding place, and they never will." He smiled.

"You must be wondering why I didn't retrieve the gold myself. Yes, I tried. Every time, I failed. I never believed in nonsense about ghosts and apparitions, but everything changed after we finished hiding the treasure and left the *Posada del Sol*. I'm convinced a curse fell on us. From that moment on, I never slept well again. The evils of my past, came to life and have haunted me ever since, like demons from hell. I think my downfall was complete when I chose to remain silent about everything I discovered. Secrets I should have revealed but didn't, out of cowardice. I became complicit in the crime." He looked crestfallen, his eyes brimming with tears.

"A few days after hiding the gold centennials, they tried to wipe us off the map. My companions weren't as lucky. They were killed mercilessly. I barely escaped, almost by divine intervention. My infamous stint at the Federal Security Directorate served me well. I knew what precautions to take. I didn't want to give them a second chance, so I fled to the United States that very day, where I hid for a year. I left everything behind like a coward. Fortunately, they stopped looking for me. The change of government came, and all of Durazo's accomplices fled. Many ended up in jail or dead. I was the least of their worries. When I returned to Mexico City, I decided to retrieve the gold centennials but failed again, partly because of my drug addiction, which had me in a pitiful state of degradation. That day, when I broke into the hotel, I was *really high*. But despite this, while I was inside that place, an irrational terror gripped me. I saw and felt things that I'm certain weren't caused by the drugs. I fled, terrified, screaming like a madman. Naturally, the guards at the place called the police, and I ended up in jail, charged with breaking and entering. My time there was brief because I had good contacts in the Attorney General's Office in the capital. After that incident, I abandoned any attempt to return. Every time I thought about it, fear coursed through my veins. I never understood why, as I had never been fearful before. In a way, I was used to feeling fear. But from that moment on, nightmares became my frequent nocturnal visitors. It wasn't until a couple of years ago that I mustered the courage to make one last attempt. I took advantage of a trip to Mexico City. I gave the matter a lot of thought and prepared myself mentally. I used the little money I had in the bank to buy some tools and bribe the security guard at the place. I didn't want to seek help; I intended to take only what I could carry. My interest at that time was no longer just about the gold, but about *something* I'm about to reveal to you. My intentions were anything but good, and as soon as I crossed the entrance gate, an unbearable pain—like nothing I had ever felt—

invaded my stomach and intestines. It was as if thousands of needles were buried in me, tearing out my insides. I writhed on the ground like a dying insect until I lost consciousness. When I came to, I was in a hospital. Leonor was by my side, and that's when she made a brutal revelation. I had undergone emergency surgery because one of my intestines had perforated. They opened me up. Diagnosis: the doctors found that my colon was infested with cancer. That's why I'm convinced that place cursed me for my criminal behavior," he said, letting out a deep sigh.

"You can't imagine how good it feels to finally be telling someone this." Martin sighed deeply.

"I insist, Braulio; I don't want you to feel obligated. The decision is yours alone. If the gold centennials cause you any moral discomfort, forget about them. And if you decide to go, focus only on the second thing buried there, which is all that matters in the end. Ignore the ghost stories. Everything I saw and suffered at the *Posada del Sol* is nothing more than the product of my black conscience. Sooner or later, guilt and regret come at you like vengeful beasts, eager to shove the past in your face and laugh while doing so. *La Posada* is like an amplifier that magnifies bad feelings in people like me. Therefore, what matters most to me is the last thing I will tell you. It will finally allow me to rest. I should have spoken out long ago. Gold is important, no doubt, but not as much as what I want you to rescue from that place." Martin paused and took a deep breath.

"Remember the double centennial joined by a hinge? It has a crucial role. I assume you've already seen it. I'll explain later in detail what the message engraved inside means. It's the key. But I don't want to get ahead of myself. I've gone on too long, and now I must be brief. Here is the revelation of the second great treasure. *Look, it turns out… once you do it, it's crucial… for you… to know… for years… many….*" At that point, the audio and video began to stutter and skip. Martin's voice became unintelligible. Braulio paused it, hoping that would fix the issue. He clicked play again from the moment of failure.

"*… Durazo… people in his charge… during… wa… dirty… unimaginable…*" The image became corrupted and pixelated until Martin looked like an 8-bit graphic. Soon, the screen went black. Immediately afterward, a warning appeared: "An unexpected error has occurred in playback," followed by a dialog box to close the video. Braulio closed it and reopened it, playing from the beginning and fast-forwarding to the point where he had left off. According to the indicator, there were only a few minutes left in the recording.

"*Look, it turns out… once you do that, it's important….*"

The warning reappeared: "An unexpected error has occurred in playback." This time the error caused Braulio's laptop to stop responding. He had to restart it. A feeling of confusion and dizziness washed over him. As the system rebooted, he mentally reviewed everything the video had revealed. He didn't know what to think. He decided to move to an armchair in the TV room. The operating system had booted up. He quickly searched for the video file and double-clicked it. His heart raced when a dialog box appeared with a sentence that felt like a death sentence: "It seems that the file is damaged and cannot be opened." He felt the breath leave his lungs.

"Damn it!" he yelled in frustration.

He closed all the open windows. He would try the traditional method to fix this kind of error—ejecting the USB and reinserting it into another port. Doing so brought up an even more ominous dialog: "USB device not recognized. Do you want to format?"

"This can't be happening! It just can't be!" he shouted, exasperated. He tried the process several times, but the result was always the same: "The USB device is not recognized. Do you want to format?" There was no way to view the video file anymore. Everything indicated that the content had been lost. Fury surged through him, and he almost slammed the laptop to the floor, but he restrained himself.

"Damn it! What do I do now?" he muttered, placing both hands on his head.

He felt extreme frustration at the thought that his uncle's revelation would be incomplete and lost forever. What was that last part that he had emphasized so much? He took a deep breath, trying to think of a solution, but nothing came to mind.

*"Poor uncle. I hope his eternal rest isn't disturbed by this—if such a thing exi*sts" he thought, consoling himself with the idea that at least his uncle had left this world believing the video would be seen in its entirety. But the same thought kept returning: *"What was that last thing he was about to reveal?"* As if fate were playing a cruel joke, Braulio would now carry that cursed doubt for the rest of his life. That uncertainty would torment him unless he decided to go to the *Posada del Sol,* not just to find the centennials but to uncover what had been left unrevealed because of a technological curse. It was maddening. He squirmed in the chair.

"Fucking piece of shit!" he yelled in frustration as he stared at the USB, realizing that it was a Chinese trinket, disposable, a generic piece of garbage. It was always the same with those generic devices you can get at any corner store. But how would his uncle know? He must have passed through quite an ordeal to record the video.

No matter how much technical knowledge he had derived from his training as an engineer, a damaged USB device was impossible to repair for all practical purposes. Besides, he wouldn't risk having it repaired and someone else seeing the video. "What if copies were made? Or worse yet, how about virilizing the information?" he thought, paranoid. He had reached a dead end.

CHAPTER 15

Braulio felt dazed; Martin's confession seemed unbelievable. For a moment, he convinced himself that the whole story was merely a delusion, a hallucination born of a dying man's terminal illness. Senile dementia, the side effects of chemo, and years of drug abuse had all compounded. It was too fanciful to be real, but somehow, the story began to acquire a strange logic and coherence. Many details aligned with other stories Martin had told. "*I don't even know what to think,*" he kept muttering to himself.

He examined the box's contents again, now understanding the facts. He took out the blueprints, which he now knew corresponded to the *Posada del Sol* hotel. He scrutinized them. The building was large, with several floors, terraces, halls, domes, open spaces, corridors, and more corridors that eventually seemed labyrinthine. It was a whimsical, strange, and confusing design. As an engineer, he could easily read the blueprints. He focused on the annotations and notes left by Martin, which outlined a route through corridors, false walls, and tunnels. *"What kind of madness was that place? Was it really a hotel?"* he wondered, frowning. He paused at the spot where Martin had marked an *X* on the map, except there were two marks, indicating two different locations, separated by a few meters. Below the first *X* was a notation that read "100," clearly referencing the centennials. The second *X* bore the word "Oblivion." This was where Martin had placed so much importance on whatever was hidden. But what could it be?

He looked again at the hinged double gold centennial, focusing on the phrase *DAMNATIO MEMORIAE*. He grabbed his phone to search the internet for its meaning. It was a Latin phrase meaning "the condemnation of memory." He discovered that it was a practice in ancient Rome, where the memory of those considered enemies of the state was condemned after their death. The Roman Senate would officially decree a *Damnatio Memoriae*, ordering the elimination, erasure, and destruction of any trace of the condemned—statues, monuments, images, and writings. They even went so far as to forbid the use of the condemned's name. At one point in history, *Damnatio Memoriae* was applied even to some emperors. Absorbed in thought, he still couldn't make sense of it.

He endured a hellish night, unable to sleep as the thoughts, especially of the *unrevealed thing*, bombarded him like a freight train. The idea of recovering the gold was undeniably tempting.

He tossed and turned in bed, contemplating calling Fabiola, but he dismissed the idea. He didn't even know where to start with such a crazy story, and besides, it was well past midnight. He didn't want to worry her. It was something to be discussed in person. Around three in the morning, he began to drift off, only for a terrible nightmare to interrupt his brief rest. He woke up, terrified. He had dreamt of his uncle Martin. They were in what appeared to be a medieval catacomb, an amorphous, indecipherable space. He heard his uncle call out to him, and when he approached, he was horrified to find Martin lying on the ground, split in two. Blood pooled everywhere, with intestines and viscera exposed, writhing as though begging for help. Braulio was paralyzed by the terrifying sight.

All around him, unintelligible voices echoed, crowded, and threatening. The scene was nightmarish. Awake now, Braulio wiped sweat from his forehead, breathing deeply. He turned on the light by his bedside. The first thing he saw was the box. He stared at it, fearing his uncle might have been right, that knowledge was indeed a curse. He tried to calm himself, knowing he was overwhelmed by everything that had happened. To clear his mind, he turned on the television and randomly chose a series until he finally fell asleep.

Thankfully, it was Friday. He would have the whole weekend to rest, think things over, and organize the mess of ideas in his mind. Braulio found it impossible to concentrate during the workday; several cups of coffee were all that kept him from falling asleep in his cubicle. He couldn't stop thinking about his uncle, *the Posada del Sol*, and the centennials.

"Will you look at that face? You must've had a great party," some of his colleagues teased sarcastically.

He arranged to meet Fabiola at his apartment as soon as he got off work to tell her everything.

"You sound worried; what did your uncle leave you? What's going on? Tell me now! At least give me a hint, but don't leave me hanging," Fabiola demanded, sensing something was off with Braulio.

"I can't explain over the phone. It's too long, and I don't want to risk any leaks. It's too important," he replied, realizing how paranoid he must have sounded.

CHAPTER 16

Fabiola arrived at Braulio's apartment at six in the evening. Although she typically left the office at seven, she justified her early departure by taking advantage of the fact that it was Friday and the law firm partners had already left. She had completed all her tasks to meet with Braulio as soon as possible.

"All right now, tell me, why so much mystery? You've had me intrigued all morning," she said, her tone both accusing and concerned.

Braulio took her by the hand and led her to the sofa. He poured two glasses of red wine, believing they could serve as an elixir: one that would help him relax and tell his story more fluidly, and another to help her digest something that might sound crazy—or like the delirium of a dying man, as he had once feared.

"Relax; this is going to take a while."

He began the narration by first showing her the contents of the box. He wished he could have shown her the video and let Martin tell the unbelievable story, but this was impossible due to a technical glitch. As he progressed through the story, he became increasingly convinced that it couldn't be a lie; the details fit together like puzzle pieces. If Fabiola hadn't already known some of Martin's anecdotes, she might have thought it all the product of a mentally unbalanced mind. But just like Braulio, all the evidence she had in hand fit together like Lego pieces. He showed her the blueprints and photographs of the *Posada del Sol*, as well as those of her uncle and other figures from the Durazo era. They leafed through the small book, and Fabiola eyed the dedication with interest.

"Did your uncle know the author?"

"Yes, according to what my uncle narrated in the video, he worked for him for a while. I've been leafing through it, and some of the anecdotes in the book match the ones my uncle used to tell."

"Quite a character, this Durazo guy. I remember my dad talking about him, mentioning something about how he ordered a palace to be built on a Mexican beach. I think it was called the Parthenon—a replica of an ancient Greek temple. Delusions of grandeur," Fabiola said, shrugging. She was surprised to see the hinged double centennial. Taking it in her hands, she realized it was solid gold. It seemed like a strange, crude object to her as she ran her fingers over the angels' faces, feeling their contours. "I've never held gold centennials before. It looks like those ostentatious decorations that drug lords are so fond of," she remarked, her eyes still fixed on the object.

Braulio nodded. "An ostentation of bad taste. The product of a megalomaniac's mind."

Fabiola opened the jewelry box and studied the inscriptions with a frown. She read aloud:

"*DAMNATIO MEMORIAE*," and after a second, she affirmed, "It's Latin."

"Do you know what it means?" Braulio asked.

"Remembering my Roman Law classes, I think it means something like *Condemnation of memory*," she replied, fixing her gaze on him.

Braulio agreed and continued explaining what he had found online about it.

"I still don't understand what this object represents. It must have something to do with the centennials. Maybe a password. It wasn't something mentioned in the video," he said, frowning slightly. "In the book I just showed you, there's a part where it's stated that Durazo sent some gold centennials to a jeweler to modify them, and they ended up in pieces like this one, used as gifts for politicians, artists, lovers, and those he wanted to impress. He was like a third-world version of King Midas. In the video, my uncle said he would explain the object's purpose.

Perhaps its only function was to prove the existence of the centennials. I don't know," he said, shaking his head.

"I can't figure out what other meaning it might have."

They lost track of time amidst all the details, and when they finally noticed, nearly three hours had passed.

"Everything you've just told me sounds incredible; it's like something out of a movie or a story about treasure hunters," Fabiola said, smiling slightly.

"Like I told you, I couldn't even sleep last night just thinking about it."

"And what do you plan to do?" Fabiola asked.

"Honestly, I have no idea. A part of me says I should seize this golden opportunity, but another warns me that it's sheer madness. Can you imagine? How and where would you start looking? I don't even know which part of Mexico City this place is in. What if it's a dangerous area? According to my uncle, it's a building that was—or still is—government property, not only abandoned but also closed to the public and under constant surveillance. My uncle ended up behind bars the last time he tried to break in. Plus, the place must be crawling with rats, all kinds of poisonous animals, and thugs who use it for all sorts of nefarious activities."

"Are you going to tell anyone else?" Fabiola asked.

"No way. This was very important to my uncle, and it's a

sacred oath I must keep and protect. I'm obligated to make good use of everything he told me. I owe it to his memory," he answered, remaining thoughtful for a moment.

"Too bad the video got lost. I'm left with such uncertainty about what was in that part that wasn't shown. My uncle said many times that it was of great importance to him, even more so than the gold coins themselves," he said, shaking his head and placing a hand on his forehead.

"I think that's what caused the nightmare I had. My conscience is reproaching me. I'm afraid it will become a subconscious suggestion that won't let me rest, you know?" he spoke with a resigned sigh.

Fabiola moved closer and hugged him. "Don't stress, babe. It wasn't your fault. The good thing is, as you said, at least your uncle was able to record the video, so he passed away believing that the message had reached you completely."

"Well…yes, I guess you're right. Believe me, if it weren't for that missing part, I could just leave this whole thing alone and keep it as a great anecdote in the same box my uncle left me. But that incomplete part tempts me to find out at all costs what that other treasure is."

They remained thoughtful, wrapped in a hug, and she snuggled into his chest.

"By the way, have you ever heard of that place?" Fabiola asked

"No, never. All I know is what my uncle told me. Beyond that, I have no idea how to find more information."

"Are you sure about that? Your uncle practically told you where to look."

"Did he?" he asked, surprised.

"Where would be the best place to find stories about abandoned and haunted places?"

CHAPTER 17

They were astonished to find more than twenty YouTube videos recounting the infamous history of the *Posada del Sol* hotel. Among enthusiasts of abandoned, mysterious, and haunted sites, the place held a certain notoriety. They stumbled upon various channels featuring content ranging from humorous and ridiculous to well-researched and informative. Their surprise deepened when they discovered the hotel had even served as a set for a horror movie. They felt like hermits in the vast digital village, suddenly exposed to a world they had never known. They watched the videos on Braulio's laptop while eating the pizzas they ordered for dinner. Mysteries of abandoned places turned out to be more entertaining than they had expected. It was the perfect way to spend a frozen Friday in January. They joked about the possibility of uploading their own video, given the remarkable story they had about the infamous hotel.

"We might even go viral," Braulio quipped.

From the videos, they learned that the *Posada del Sol* was located in the Doctores neighborhood of Mexico City. Built in the early 1940s, it was intended to become the city's most important and impressive hotel, as well as a cultural center meant to attract artists and intellectuals from around the world. Grand events would be held to draw presidents, prime ministers, kings, princes, and various dignitaries. The name "Sol," meaning "sun," symbolized how its doors would welcome people with a brightness comparable to that of the solar star. This extravagant and ambitious architectural work blended various styles, from Baroque and classical to avant-garde and abstract forms without apparent meaning. It opened its doors in 1945 but only operated for eight months. The reasons for its closure, as narrated in the videos, were often contradictory and steeped in fantasy.

They noted that the hotel was a bizarre, capricious, enigmatic, and incomprehensible structure, just as Braulio had seen in the blueprints and photographs left by his uncle. It housed five hundred rooms spread across several buildings. Murals, monoliths, anthropomorphic sculptures—many of which felt eerie—along with courtyards, gardens, a theater, an auditorium, and even a chapel, adorned the place.

The hotel's owner and creator, architect Fernando Saldaña Galván, was a figure shrouded in mystery. According to the videos, he had fallen into disgrace due to the enormous debts incurred by the project. Other stories mentioned conspiracies, vendettas, and legal issues stemming from the mismanagement of public funds, or rivalries between political factions, and even Masonic plots. Despite being a wealthy man, Saldaña had also dabbled in politics and had once served as mayor of Mexico City. One account claimed the architect took his own life within the hotel, hanging himself from a bell tower, unable to bear the pressures as his magnum opus turned against him like a rabid animal. There were rumors of dark forces behind his downfall, with some even suggesting he was murdered. Other versions claimed that every day at a particular hour—coinciding with the time of his alleged suicide—the bell would ring inside the hotel, heralding the spectral procession of Saldaña and an entourage of tormented souls. However, in a contradictory twist, another version of Saldaña's fate suggested he died of old age, in obscurity and poverty, abandoned in his home. All the tales about the hotel bordered on the fantastical, but one story, in particular, aligned somewhat with the version his uncle had narrated.

One video mentioned that during the tenure of *Negro* Durazo as head of the General Directorate of Police and Traffic in the Federal District, now Mexico City, he had allegedly used the hotel as a clandestine operations center for all sorts of atrocities, from storing drugs and stolen goods to hosting orgies and bacchanals. The *Posada del Sol* was perfect for such activities since it was owned by the city government and abandoned. Some residents of the surrounding areas claimed to hear screams, moans, and cries at night, with others attributing these to satanic rituals. Braulio felt a strange tightening in his chest as he realized his uncle had ventured into the bowels of this place to hide secrets known only to them. Now everything made sense. There was no doubt that the centennials were hidden in the secret tunnels of the *Posada del Sol*, along with whatever else his uncle had deemed more important. But what could possibly be more valuable than several hundred gold coins? What kind of unspeakable secret lay buried there?

Fabiola decided to stay the night with Braulio since it was past midnight by the time they noticed the hour. They both needed each other's company, feeling a bit like children who, after watching a scary movie, don't want to sleep alone. Although neither would admit it, the stories had unsettled them, especially Braulio. He didn't know what to think or what to do next. Should he fulfill Martin's request to find the treasures? Under the sheets, they discussed the matter until they both drifted off to sleep.

CHAPTER 18

Saturday morning. They woke up late, exchanging tender morning greetings as lovers do. They got up and prepared breakfast. Braulio felt aches in his body, especially in his neck—likely the effects of stress. They turned on a small gas heater to warm the kitchen, as it was bitterly cold. During breakfast, Braulio seemed distant and preoccupied.

"Honey, are you okay? You're somewhere else; I was asking you something."

Braulio snapped out of his reverie. "Yes, babe," he replied, shaking his head. "Sorry, I was lost in thought about all this. I've been mulling it over, and I think I've made my decision."

"Really?" Fabiola asked, taking his hand.

"Look, this whole thing is insane. While it seems the gold centennials are hidden as my uncle described and I have the means to find them, the idea of entering that place is just madness. For starters, how would I even do it? I'd have to bypass the security or, at best, bribe the guards to let me in. Even if I managed that, what would I say to justify my presence? I'd need tools—shovels, picks, who knows what else—to break down walls and dig. What would I tell the guards? *Hey there, I'm Braulio; I'll just be a minute, just looking for some treasure, and I'll be on my way,*" he mocked. They both burst into laughter.

"Even if I overcame that first hurdle, there's the possibility of encountering others inside. We saw how many people sneak in to make their documentaries and videos for the internet. But what about those who don't post their adventures? We're not considering the possibility of running into those lunatics who throw secret parties, use drugs, or conduct satanic rituals. We can't dismiss that."

Fabiola laughed. "Aren't you exaggerating a bit, babe?" Braulio smiled.

"Well, we don't know," he said. "But seriously, there's a real danger of being accused of breaking and entering, like what happened to my uncle, and of theft. As a lawyer, what's your take on that?"

"Well, if the hotel is government-owned or privately held, everything inside it belongs to the rightful owner, including the gold. So, yes, there's a strong chance you could be charged with theft," Fabiola explained. Braulio frowned slightly.

"Even if I found the centennials and got out unnoticed, another problem arises: how do I transport them? My uncle mentioned there are around seventeen thousand coins. I couldn't possibly carry that many. Even just a saddlebag would be a challenge. There's no way around it; I'd need help, which means involving others. Completely out of the question."

"I could help you. Or are you not planning to share your riches with me?" Fabiola teased, frowning and smiling.

"Of course I am, babe; what's mine is yours," he replied with a dramatic flourish.

"Liar!" she said with mock anger, and then they kissed.

"Breaking walls would make noise, which could attract anyone else inside. What if they show up right when I strike gold? I doubt anyone would offer me selfless and kind support. There's a high chance my sad skeleton would become part of the hotel. Just another tale: *Today, we tell the story of the man who sought treasure and found only death at the hands of thieves. Now, he wanders the hotel's halls, searching for lost gold centennials.* Good material for a YouTube video." They both laughed.

"But then there's the other mysterious treasure. My uncle's words, *more important than the gold*, create more unease in me than the idea of entering the hotel."

He fell silent, and they both grew pensive. Braulio stared at the table, making his decision. Fabiola watched him.

"I've decided it's best to forget about it. It's too risky; looking at the bigger picture, it's sheer madness. It would be like breaking into a museum to rob it."

"Well, in a way, yes," Fabiola agreed.

"I know it's a lot of money, and the temptation is great; as my uncle said, it could change our lives, but at what cost?" After a few seconds, he added, "And still, I feel conflicted because I'm breaking a promise," he said, raising his hand to his forehead.

"I don't see it that way, Braulio. You told me your uncle gave you a choice. He said he would respect whatever decision you made and trusted your judgment," Fabiola reminded him. Her words seemed to comfort Braulio.

"You're right," he nodded, taking Fabiola's hands.

"I'll keep the items my uncle left me and his story. Some things are better left alone."

"Haven't you thought about contacting your cousin and telling him?"

"It crossed my mind briefly, but it wouldn't be wise. If my uncle didn't do it, I don't have the right to. I wouldn't want to show up out of nowhere and tell him this crazy story. I don't want to be the one to tarnish the small, positive image he might have of my uncle, leaving him thinking he was not only a lousy father but also mentally unstable. This was entrusted to me, and it's up to me to decide. That's how my uncle arranged it. I'll choose to keep what Martin Robledo revealed to me a secret, ensuring it doesn't fall into the wrong hands. I'll preserve the plans and other relics he left me as a testament to his history, and who knows, maybe someday there will be a way to retrieve those treasures. But it won't keep me awake at night because, even though my uncle said that gold belongs to no one, it doesn't belong to us either." They both sat in silence, reflecting.

"Haven't you considered going to the authorities? Maybe they could take the necessary steps to recover the treasure and find whatever else is hidden there. That gold could become the nation's property and, in this case, perhaps be distributed to the neediest. I don't know; in some way, it could be put to good use," Fabiola suggested.

Braulio laughed bitterly. "For God's sake, are you serious? That would be like handing the treasure to criminals. The government and the thieves are one and the same in this country, where no one respects the law. The centennials would end up in the pockets of the officials in charge of the discovery."

"I sounded really naive, didn't I?"

"You're a lawyer, right?" Braulio teased, and they both burst out laughing.

CHAPTER 19

March arrived, bringing warmer weather to the city as the intense winter cold finally began to wane. Braulio found himself thinking less and less about his uncle's secret, though it proved challenging to put it out of his mind completely. Occasionally, strange ideas surfaced, often as a result of the bizarre dreams that plagued him. For weeks, he managed to push these thoughts aside, resuming a semblance of normalcy, until the strange dreams returned, more frequent and intense, evolving into nightmares. Every one of them centered on the *Posada del Sol* hotel, where he found himself wandering through blood-soaked corridors, haunted by anguished voices. In one particularly vivid dream, Braulio heard a persistent banging against a wall. As he moved closer, he could distinguish a voice, desperately calling his name from the other side.

"Braulio, get me out of here!" the voice pleaded. Braulio pressed his ear against the wall to listen more closely. "Braulio!

Please, get me out!" He recognized the voice.

"Uncle?"

"Get me out of here!" Braulio frantically searched the floor and found a pickaxe.

"Hold on, Uncle! I'm getting you out!" he shouted, filled with urgency. But as he struck the wall, a scream of intense pain reverberated through the space, as though the wall itself were alive. Before he could react, the wall collapsed on him, crushing him with terrifying force.

He awoke drenched in sweat, gasping for breath. Thankfully, Fabiola was there that night, it being the weekend, and she helped calm him, providing comfort in her embrace.

The worst nightmare, however, occurred when he was alone, forcing him to sleep with the light on, like a frightened child. In this dream, he found himself in the hotel gardens, unable to tell if it was day or night. He sensed something—a presence, an amorphous entity—chasing him. He ran frantically, with a bell tolling in the distance. The closer he got to the source of the sound, the more dread consumed him. He spotted a post with a bell hanging in the air. As he approached, he froze upon realizing that a person was hanging from the post. At first, the figure was indistinct, but as he drew nearer, he recognized his uncle's face. Suddenly, his uncle's eyes opened, revealing two enormous, hollow sockets.

"Get me out of here!" his uncle screamed.

Using these nightmarish experiences as an excuse, Fabiola decided to move into Braulio's apartment. The companionship, they believed, would help him manage his fears. However, this was not a new discussion; they had already considered living together, believing their relationship held great promise. Fabiola, still living with her parents at twenty-nine, felt it was high time to strike out on her own. Her presence at night eased Braulio's nightmares, making them less frequent. Sharing breakfasts in the morning before work, and dinners in the evening while watching television series, helped distract him from what they jokingly referred to as a cursed inheritance. The two of them relished each other's company.

CHAPTER 20

It was a Tuesday in early April. Braulio and Fabiola went to bed shortly after dinner, feeling exhausted. Both had endured a rather unpleasant workday. Braulio slept peacefully until he was disturbed by noises in his dreams—perhaps footsteps. He found himself in what seemed to be the enormous entrance hall of an opulent place. The details were obscured by darkness, but the presence of others was palpable, causing his heart to race. He glimpsed shadows approaching, and his heart sank—the nightmares were back. A hand suddenly rested on his shoulder, jolting him awake. Fabiola had shaken him.

"What's happening?" Braulio asked, disoriented and agitated.

"I think I heard something," she whispered.

Braulio listened. At first, there was only silence, then the faint sound of a chair moving. It was quiet but unmistakable. They both held their breath, paralyzed by adrenaline—another noise. Fabiola clung tightly to Braulio's arm. The sounds couldn't be from a pet; they didn't have one. Nor could they be from a relative, as no one else had a key. The noises were definitely coming from inside the apartment. Braulio checked the time on his cell phone: 2:13 a.m. He decided to investigate, despite Fabiola's urging him to call 911. He reassured her, insisting there must be a logical explanation. Taking his cell phone, he turned on the flashlight, avoiding turning on the lights fully. He moved cautiously toward the bedroom door. Fabiola sat up in bed, anxiously watching him. Braulio walked down a short hallway leading to the dining room. The silence was heavy, and everything seemed in order until, without warning, a shadow materialized and struck him in the face. Braulio fell forward, unable to react—it all happened in an instant. He momentarily lost consciousness and felt someone's knees pressing into his back, another holding his hands behind him. It felt like an arrest, but instead of handcuffs, they used what he assumed was duct tape.

Fabiola had heard the thud and instinctively clung to the sheets.

"Braulio! What was that noise?" she yelled. No response, just more noises. Panic set in, and she began to tremble.

"Braulio!" she called out again. Footsteps and muffled voices grew louder as they neared the bedroom.

Fabiola's survival instinct kicked in. She leaped out of bed, rushing to close and lock the door. Instantly, someone began pounding on it, the slamming escalating in desperation.

"Open the door, or you're gonna fucking regret it!" an unfamiliar male voice shouted.

Fabiola was paralyzed with fear, unable to speak or think clearly. Her first instinct was to find her cell phone, but it wasn't on the nightstand where she thought she had left it. The person outside the door was banging louder and louder.

"Open the damn door!" he demanded angrily.

Fabiola scrambled onto the bed and finally found her phone. She tried frantically to unlock it and call the police, but before she could, the door burst open with a violent kick. She froze as a masked intruder in black lunged at her, subduing her quickly. She could do little to resist as he silenced her screams with a strip of duct tape.

Fabiola and Braulio were violently thrown onto the sofa in the living room. A small lamp on a nearby table illuminated the scene. Both had their hands tied behind their backs, and duct tape sealed their mouths. Braulio, still dazed from the blow, quickly regained his senses when he saw Fabiola gagged and terrified, tears streaming down her face. She struggled desperately to free herself. Braulio tried to calm her with a look, but they could only emit muffled moans.

Three men stood before them. Two of them pointed guns directly at Braulio and Fabiola. The first man was tall, about six feet, and muscular, dressed in tactical black clothing. He was the one who had subdued them. The second man was a stark contrast, short and obese, dressed like a Mexican country singer—plaid shirt, large belt buckle, exotic leather boots, and Wrangler-style pants. He was the most verbally abusive of the three. The third man had a more ordinary build, medium height and slim, dressed in a dark turtleneck and old-fashioned dress pants. He sat calmly in a chair facing the couple, with the other two flanking him. Without a doubt, he was the leader. All three men wore balaclavas, and the smell of tobacco and alcohol clung to them. Fabiola continued to writhe and cry.

"Calm down, bitch!" the obese man yelled.

Braulio tried to stand, but the muscular man pressed the gun against him more firmly. "Calm down, dude, or you lose your fucking head—literally."

The leader intervened to deescalate the situation.

"Let's all calm down, shall we? The more you cooperate, the sooner this is over. No need for violence, right, little friend?" he said, addressing Braulio. Braulio nodded and turned to Fabiola, making signs and facial expressions to urge her to calm down. From all the crime dramas and detective shows he had watched, Braulio knew that the best thing to do in this situation was to remain composed, not to play the hero. At least in fiction, it often worked. They both stayed still.

"Well, well, that's how things are done," the leader said in an almost priestly tone.

"As you may have guessed by now, we're here to take a few things—preferably of good value, fine quality, if you know what I mean. From what we've seen, you're a young couple with no kids. You seem well-educated, probably with good jobs, which leads us to believe you have a taste for the finer things. And people like you probably have decent savings in the bank." He ended the sentence with a cynical smirk.

Braulio quickly deduced two things. First, they had been watched and investigated beforehand, indicating these were likely professional thieves. Second, the leader's manner of speaking suggested he was not just any thug but someone with some education, possibly even police training. He addressed others with authority, exhibiting a certain command and discipline. In Mexico, it wasn't uncommon for the police to moonlight as thieves. The entire country was engulfed in a wave of rampant insecurity.

"Look, little friend, I'm going to let you talk so you can tell me what I need to know. The quicker you cooperate, the quicker this ends, don't you think?"

Braulio nodded.

The man approached and violently ripped the duct tape from Braulio's mouth. Braulio winced as the tape tore away some of his facial hair, causing the muscular man to chuckle. Fabiola, far from calming down, felt even more terrified as the two burly men stared at her with undisguised lust. The only part of their faces visible beneath their balaclavas were their eyes and mouths, both filled with lecherous intent. Fabiola, dressed only in a small nightgown and thong, was practically naked. With her hands bound, she could do little to cover herself, leaving her exposed beauty all too apparent. Realizing this, Braulio's urgency intensified.

"Take what you want; I'll give you everything, just please don't hurt my girlfriend," he begged.

The big man and his rotund companion laughed. Their leader replied, "Well, it's up to you, little friend."

Braulio revealed the location of his laptop, a latest-generation desktop Mac, and various other valuables, including some designer watches. They weren't luxury items, but they had good market value. He emphasized the latest-generation Apple Watch he owned and pointed them to a spot in his closet where he kept around forty thousand pesos in cash.

"That sounds pretty good... unreported cash," the leader said, as the other two burst out laughing.

"How big is that screen?" the burly man asked, waving his gun.

"Sixty-five inches," Braulio answered.

"We're taking it along with that PS5 console," he said, grinning.

The corpulent men began to load up the stolen goods while

the leader kept an eye on Braulio and Fabiola. Braulio immediately thought of the security cameras in the hallways and parking lot. It seemed as if the leader had read his mind, as he now pointed the gun directly at them.

"I wouldn't worry about the cameras, little friend; they're going to need replacing," he said, letting out a quiet chuckle. The way he kept saying *little friend* made Braulio's blood boil.

"So, you're an engineer, and your girlfriend is a lawyer. An unusual couple, isn't it? Usually, you find couples where both are lawyers or one is a lawyer and the other an accountant."

Braulio didn't know how to respond; at that moment, the comment felt utterly ridiculous. He simply shrugged. The leader fell silent and turned his gaze to Fabiola. She felt harassed, wishing she could scream, "Stop looking at me, you filthy pig!" The leader released a sardonic smile and focused on Braulio again.

"Anything else to declare, little friend?" he asked, like a customs inspector, his gaze piercing.

Braulio couldn't help but think of the double gold centennial his uncle had given him, but he told himself that he would never reveal that to these vile thieves. As soon as they got their hands on the gold coin, they would start asking more questions. One thing would lead to another. Luckily, he had hidden it in a wooden box, secured in a false bottom in his closet, under a corner where he kept his shoes. The leader eyed him suspiciously, waiting for an answer.

"The only thing I have left is my car. Other than that, it's just the money in my account. I don't own anything else," Braulio said.

The leader approached him. "The car is useless to us, but how much money are we talking about?"

Braulio lied about the amount, assuming the thieves would settle for whatever they could withdraw from the ATM, which was usually limited to ten thousand pesos per day. They wouldn't be able to get more later, as their cards would be canceled, and the theft reported.

"How much money does your pretty girlfriend have?"

"I don't know," he answered, glancing at her.

"Don't worry; we'll find out soon enough. I imagine you have online banking, right?" Braulio felt nervous. He hesitated. By then, the other two men had already removed the loot from the apartment. The leader ordered the fat one to confiscate their cell phones and then turned to Braulio.

"Give me your passwords to unlock and access online banking."

Braulio started to stutter. Nervously, he confused letters and numbers, struggling to give the correct information. Eventually, the leader managed to access Braulio's account, his mouth twisting into a sneer of surprise.

"You lied about the amount. There's more money here. Why

are you messing with me?" the leader asked coldly.

"Well... how much is there?" Braulio stammered.

The leader responded with a hard punch to his right cheek, finishing with a kick to his stomach. Braulio doubled over in pain, gasping for air. Fabiola began to moan and kick in desperation. The corpulent man subdued her.

"Don't worry, darling, he'll be fine," he said lustfully, taking the opportunity to grope her.

Almost a minute passed before Braulio began to recover from the beating.

"First and last time you try to be clever with me, little friend. Next time, I'll shoot you in the balls. Is that clear?" the leader shouted. Braulio nodded, trembling with fear and pain.

"Excuse me, I'm very nervous. I got confused," he replied in a broken voice. The burly man was still holding Fabiola.

"Let her go," the leader ordered. "He's going to behave himself, right?" he said, addressing Braulio.

"Look, little friend, here's what we're going to do. You're going to transfer money from your account and your girlfriend's account to this one," he said, showing him a cell phone screen displaying a QR code for immediate transfers.

"It's an untraceable account. Cryptocurrencies so don't get your hopes up. There's no way to know who the owner is. The wonders of technology and the blockchain," he said smugly.

He manipulated Braulio's phone, scanned the QR code, and

asked for the bank confirmation password.

"That was fast! See?" said the leader, smiling.

An intense sadness overwhelmed Braulio, followed by anger. Years of savings were gone. His plans, if any still existed, were now shattered. Why was this happening to them? Everything had happened so fast; he hadn't even realized how much danger they were in. He didn't know how this nightmare would end. Thoughts of his parents and the religiosity his mother had instilled in him flooded his mind. He found it ironic that this might be useful now. He entrusted himself to God. He couldn't hold back the tears.

"Oh, look, the little gentleman is crying," the fat man mocked. The burly man laughed.

"What's your girlfriend going to say?"

"What's she going to say? That she has a queer for a boyfriend," the corpulent man burst out laughing.

"Enough! Keep quiet, you two idiots. Our friends here are behaving. All that's left is to transfer the funds from this beautiful lady's account, and we'll be done. I'm going to remove the tape from your mouth. But you must promise not to do anything stupid, like scream. Will you behave?" the leader asked, pointing his index finger at her. She nodded.

The leader repeated the same process with Fabiola's accounts to transfer the money. She was sobbing, tears streaming down her face. Braulio felt helpless, unable to comfort her with a hug.

The leader leaned back in his chair, still facing Braulio and Fabiola. The other two men flanked him, resuming their positions. He seemed pensive, watching them with a slight frown. An awkward silence filled the room. It felt like an eternity to Fabiola. Braulio silently prayed for those bastards to leave.

"Well, gentlemen, I think we're done. There's nothing else we're interested in, so..." he said, standing up from the chair. The other two prepared to move. "Although..." the three paused, "I think we want something else. It's too good to pass up," the leader said.

He looked at his cronies. They smiled knowingly and fixed their eyes on Fabiola. She realized their intentions immediately. Their leering gazes said more than a thousand words. Panic set in. Braulio also guessed what was about to happen. Before Fabiola could scream, the burly man swiftly covered her mouth with duct tape again. Braulio tried to get up, but the obese man stopped him with a decisive blow to the ribs, leaving him immobilized and collapsing to the ground. The big man grabbed Fabiola. The fat man approached and ripped off her nightgown.

"Would you look at that? Damn! You look so good, baby," he said with extreme lust, almost bestially, as he stared at her breasts. He began unbuttoning his pants. Fabiola moaned in terror.

The leader ordered her to be taken to the bedroom. Braulio,

still paralyzed, felt helpless. He didn't know what to do until, as if by magic, the phrase *Damnatio Memoriae* flashed in his mind. He knew it.

"Wait! Wait! Don't do it, there's..." he shouted desperately, but couldn't finish his plea as the leader kicked him in the stomach. The burly man slung Fabiola over his shoulder like a sack and headed for the bedroom, followed by the obese man.

"There's gold! Centennials!" Braulio stammered; his words barely intelligible as he struggled to breathe. The leader turned to face him.

"What did you say?"

"Gold...!"

"I don't understand you! Explain yourself!" he yelled in exasperation.

"There's more gold than you can imagine!"

CHAPTER 21

The leader ordered the corpulent man and the obese one to stop. He turned to Braulio, approached, grabbed him by the shirt, and yanked him into the chair.

"Let's see, what are you talking about? What gold?"

"Hundreds of gold centennials could be yours, but I'll give them to you only if you don't harm my girlfriend. Don't touch her; let her go. I demand that commitment in exchange for riches!" Braulio declared, locking eyes with the leader.

The leader eyed him suspiciously. "This better not be a trick. Otherwise, we'll find another way to hurt your little girlfriend," he snarled, pointing the gun barrel at Braulio.

"No, it's not a trick. There are seventeen thousand gold centennials hidden in one place. I know where they are and how you can easily find them. But we need to make a deal. I'll give you all the necessary information, but you must leave my girlfriend alone. That's all I ask."

"It better not be a trap because if it is, we'll fill you with lead. Speak now," the leader demanded.

Braulio had no choice. The circumstances forced him to reveal Martin Robledo's secret to these vulgar criminals. It was his last resort, a desperate plea. At that moment, Fabiola's safety was more important. Martin's wishes were secondary. Not all the gold in the world could repair the damage that gang rape would inflict on Fabiola. In the end, that ill-gotten gold would end up in someone's hands. They would return home. There was no need to think about it. She mattered more than those cursed centennials. Braulio tried to organize his thoughts. He didn't know where to begin. He sought a way to be as precise and convincing as possible. Otherwise, the leader of these damned thieves could consider it a scam, ending badly for them.

He began the story, omitting trivial details and getting straight to the point. At the *Posada del Sol* hotel, *Negro* Durazo's accomplices had hidden those gold centennials by express order, the product of numerous extortions. Braulio had something akin to a treasure map. The hotel was in Mexico City. Before he could continue, the leader and the burly man burst out laughing.

"Gold and a *treasure map*, huh?" The leader shook his head.

"You son of a bitch! Couldn't you come up with a better story?" he growled, readying his gun.

"Say goodbye to your girlfriend."

"Wait! I can prove I'm not lying," Braulio pleaded desperately.

"I heard rumors about that hotel—that *Negro* Durazo used it as some sort of barracks or something," the obese man interrupted, a thoughtful expression crossing his face. The leader turned to look at him. "At least I know that hotel exists."

The leader pondered for a moment, then focused on Braulio, demanding to see the supposed proof. Braulio told him about the wooden box and where it was hidden. The leader ordered the burly man to place Fabiola back on the couch and bring her something to cover herself with. A few minutes later, the man returned with the box in hand. He handed it to the leader, who inspected it carefully. Braulio described the double gold coin inside a small black felt bag—irrefutable proof of his claim. The other two men pulled up chairs, sitting on either side, their eyes gleaming with greed as they focused on the gold.

The leader signaled the big man to hand Fabiola something to cover herself. She was still sobbing. He helped her put on a shirt he had taken from the room. It belonged to Braulio, so it fit her like a dress, which she greatly appreciated. Soon, they stopped paying attention to her. Braulio concentrated on the description, now focusing on the interpretation of the hotel blueprints that revealed the exact location of the treasure. He showed the photographs and pointed out the characters in them, including his uncle, Martin. He provided every last detail, including another secret that might also be of great value, although he had no idea what it was. It wasn't wise to keep that part to himself since there was a note on the map. He already knew the consequences of lying. Besides, what difference would it make? Perhaps Martin's entire story was symbolic, and the real hidden treasure was Fabiola's safety.

After weeks of pondering Martin's secret, Braulio had managed to piece everything together perfectly, and the story he told these damned thieves was flawless—utterly believable. When Braulio finished, the three men remained silent. They were stunned, just as he had been when he first heard the story. They were processing all the information that initially seemed like a fable but ended up making all the sense in the world. It was clear they were excited.

The three of them stood up and huddled in a corner, never taking their eyes off them. Braulio and Fabiola felt uneasy; a great uncertainty overwhelmed them. Braulio didn't know if his plan had worked and whether they would honor the deal to spare Fabiola. After a while, the three returned to their positions. The leader approached Braulio and pointed the gun at him. A horrible chill ran down his spine. Fabiola fell silent, turning pale. They thought it was all over.

"Why the hell didn't you tell us about this little secret from the beginning?" the leader demanded, his tone accusatory. Braulio paled, unsure of what to say. The leader narrowed his eyes and gave a brief smile.

"This is what we're going to do, little friend. Your story seems quite believable, but it's still subject to verification. We're going to search for *Negro* Durazo's treasure, and we better find it. For now, we'll let you go without harming your sweetie. And most importantly, you'll save yourself from getting lead in your ass," he said, letting out a laugh that was immediately echoed by the others.

"But to ensure you don't try anything funny, we're going to take precautions. I'm taking your girlfriend's phone," he stated coldly.

"Untie them," he ordered the big man.

Their hands were numb and sore. Fabiola immediately threw herself into Braulio's arms, hugging him tightly. The leader smiled and handed Fabiola a notebook and a pencil.

"Pay close attention, sweetheart. Here, you'll write down every one of your passwords, app access codes, and emails. Also, write down the full names of your parents, siblings, and their addresses. Both of you will give me your IDs. If you change your passwords, report the phone as stolen, or cancel the number, it will be the worst mistake of your lives. Any of you!" he threatened, pointing his finger at them with menacing eyes. They both nodded.

"Know this. We're top people. We're very well connected. We have ties to the police high command. If you do something stupid, no matter how minor, we'll not only come for you but also your families. If this is a trap, we'll kill them all." The almost diabolical gazes of the three men bore into the victims. Afterward, the leader took Braulio's phone and unlocked it. He manipulated it for a while. Braulio assumed he was cloning it or something like that. It was evident the leader was tech-savvy.

"All set," he said, tossing the phone back to Braulio.

"We'll be watching you closely. Don't even think about doing anything stupid," he warned, his tone menacing.

"When we find the centennials, you'll hear from us. Until then, behave yourselves. We'll know if you report us," he said, letting out a laugh that sounded quite sinister.

"Mind if I take your little memory box?"

"Not at all," Braulio answered weakly.

The leader took the photographs and the small book. He glanced at them disdainfully before tossing them back to Braulio.

"Keep them as a souvenir. I'm not interested in those old geezers," the leader sneered at the end with a mocking laugh.

They got up and left just as they had arrived. Braulio and Fabiola hugged each other tightly and cried as they had never done before until they were utterly exhausted.

CHAPTER 22

It wasn't until the following Monday, two minutes before midnight, that they received a terrifying, yet even more disconcerting, call. Fabiola and Braulio had endured six hellish days since that fateful night when the three criminals had robbed them not only of their material possessions but also of their peace and mental stability. Fabiola couldn't return to work for the rest of the week. She was too terrified to even step out into the hallway of Braulio's apartment. She pleaded with him not to leave her alone for a moment, so to justify their absences from work, they claimed to have contracted COVID-19. The doctor recommended complete rest and sufficient time to avoid spreading the virus. This way, they both explained their dull and sickly tone when speaking with friends and family. "Is something wrong? You sound a bit off," friends and family would say.

The worry and fear they felt were disguised as illness. Despite this, they managed to do some work from Braulio's apartment whenever their limited concentration allowed. Fabiola claimed to have lost her phone, adding that she still hoped to find it, which is why she hadn't reported it as lost or stolen. Perhaps she had left it in a client's office. As soon as she fully recovered, she would go looking for it. They were trapped in a prison of fear, uncertainty, confusion, and helplessness.

What tormented Braulio the most was the inability to report the criminals and take action against them, on top of having to endure text messages, mocking, and threatening calls, initially from the leader of the thugs. He had informed them that they were already in Mexico City and would soon come looking for the centennials. If they couldn't find them, Braulio should organize a *last will* among their relatives because they would all be killed.

At first, Braulio was terrified by the threats, but as the days passed, his fear turned into rage, especially when, on Monday morning, starting from eleven o'clock, he began receiving text messages from Fabiola's phone. The first message was a sarcastic compliment: "Your beauty captivated me, sweetheart." As the hours went by, the messages became more vulgar and sexually explicit. They escalated into lengthy, incoherent sexual fantasies, where the sender professed an insane love for Fabiola, speaking as if he were her lover. Two messages were particularly disturbing: one was a string of meaningless words, as if written by a madman, and the other chillingly stated, "We found the gold, my love. We're rich. See you soon." He shuddered. Had they really found it?

Would they come back for them? Braulio chose not to tell Fabiola because it would shatter her already fragile emotional state.

That night, to distract themselves, they sat on the sofa to watch the Harry Potter saga, their favorite, which always lifted their spirits. Fortunately, the messages stopped, and they finally had some peace. As Braulio held Fabiola in his arms, seeing her so helpless and terrified, he knew a final decision had to be made.

If the last message about the centennials was true, it would be foolish for the criminals to risk losing the gold just to harm them. What would be the point? If he were in their place, he would disappear without a trace. But since one can never predict a criminal's mind, it was best to be prepared. He considered acquiring a firearm, waiting for them, and unleashing a storm of bullets as soon as they set foot inside the door.

"What kind of nonsense am I thinking?" he said to himself, putting his hand to his forehead. He was distraught. They should have filed a complaint and requested police protection from the beginning. The decision was made. They would do that first thing Tuesday morning. He felt relieved until a call came through on his cell phone. The screen showed an incoming call from "Fabiola." They both froze. An intense cold ran through his veins. They felt a strange sensation in their chests. What the hell

do they want now? Fabiola clung to him tightly. Braulio thought about ignoring the call but quickly realized it was a bad idea. The dread he felt compelled him to answer. What he heard left him paralyzed and perplexed. Fabiola saw the expression on his face as Braulio held the cell phone in his hands, motionless.

"What's happening? What did they say?" she asked.

Braulio couldn't articulate a word. She shook him to make him respond. He finally told her what he heard on the other end of the line: "*Help us! They're slaughtering us! Please...!*" a voice begged, followed by a terrible scream, drowned out by blood-curdling laughter and strange noises.

They were both in shock. The first thought that crossed their minds was that it was a sick joke, an attempt to subject them to psychological terror. But to what end? What would they gain from it? Braulio checked the call log. The incoming call was at 11:58 p.m. from Fabiola's phone. They were baffled. They didn't know what to make of it or what to do. They just sat there, motionless, waiting for the phone to ring again, expecting the thugs to mock them and launch a new series of threats, now that they had the gold in hand. What if they showed up at Braulio's apartment to kill them tomorrow? It made perfect sense. Why leave witnesses who were a potential threat? They could report them at any moment, including the theft of gold from a government-owned property like *Posada del Sol*. It would immediately put all the police forces in the country on alert.

They both panicked. Fabiola burst into tears. Braulio paced around the living room, sweating, running his hands through his hair.

"We have to disappear, run away!" Fabiola cried, on the verge of hysteria.

Braulio took a deep breath. Let's calm down. We need to think things through, he thought. He sat down next to her, hugged her, and said, "What if the police found them inside the hotel? Trapped, they opened fire, and the police responded with full force and, in effect, slaughtered them."

It was the only logical explanation he could come up with.

"Could be," Fabiola replied, a bit calmer.

"I'm going to call them back." We need to find out what this is all about, if it's a joke or not. "If the police were involved, an officer would answer. If so, we'll tell them everything. What do you think?"

Fabiola nodded. He took a deep breath, unlocked the screen, and dialed the number. *Dead.* The call didn't even ring. No voicemail. He tried several times with the same result. They waited two hours after receiving the call and tried again. The line was still dead.

"Maybe there was a confrontation with the police, and they were killed on the spot," Fabiola said, frowning.

"And what if it wasn't the police who slaughtered them?"

"What are you talking about?"

"My uncle used to tell stories about a dark force that made him writhe in pain. Maybe there's something in that place. The videos we watched talk about ghosts and demonic presences. What if they were the ones who massacred them?" he said with a shrug.

"That's crazy," she replied, shaking her head.

"You're right; I'm not thinking clearly. I'm very nervous."

He made one last attempt to call. The line was dead. It was past three in the morning. They were exhausted. They decided to try to rest and file the complaint first thing in the morning. They went to bed, and for the first time since the nightmare began, they managed to enjoy a sound sleep, as if a comforting blanket had covered them.

CHAPTER 23

Braulio opened his eyes, and sunlight filtered abundantly through the blinds, illuminating the room. He was momentarily disoriented, then grabbed his watch from the bedside table and was startled to see that it was after nine in the morning. They had slept deeply and for a long time. Fabiola was still sound asleep, and he didn't want to disturb her. He got up and went to the dining room, where he prepared a cup of coffee. The first thing he did was check his cell phone for any new messages or missed calls. There were none. Without dwelling on it, he decided to make one last attempt to call. The result was the same as a few hours before.

"Honey!" Fabiola called out to him.

"Here I am."

He returned to the bedroom and told her about his latest attempt to make contact. They both agreed that the situation was strange. They speculated on a few possibilities, including the most logical one: having found the gold, the thugs might have decided to disappear. However, they both felt that the more plausible explanation was that the police had arrested them. It was unlikely that the men could have gone unnoticed in that place, especially after they had to destroy part of the building to find the centennials, which must have made a lot of noise. Braulio and Fabiola concluded that the thieves had been caught, which explained the desperate call.

Later, Braulio decided to take a bath while Fabiola prepared breakfast. They planned to go to the prosecutor's office to file a complaint once they were done. Braulio was drying off when Fabiola's shout startled him.

"Braulio! Come quickly!" she cried out.

His chest tightened as he quickly tied the towel around his waist and ran to the kitchen. He found her sitting at the table, pale, holding Braulio's tablet.

"What's going on?" he asked, concerned.

"You've got to see this!" she said urgently.

"What is it?"

"It's the news. You need to see it."

Fabiola's expression was one of utter disbelief as she stared at the screen. It was a report published on the *National Informer* website, a newspaper with national circulation.

The headline read: "Ghoulish Find. Brutally Tortured! Three Lifeless Bodies Discovered in the Drains of the Tula River." The article included a video featuring a young journalist, neatly dressed in a suit and tie, narrating the events while images and photographs related to the story appeared on the screen. Speaking more like a show host than a news anchor, he reported, "The Mexico City police announced that the discovery occurred at dawn on Tuesday. A night guard stumbled upon the bodies, which bore signs of apparent torture. The guard, upon notifying the police, stated that it was the most horrific thing he had ever seen. Forensic personnel arrived at the scene to conduct the necessary examinations and collect the bodies. According to preliminary autopsy reports, to which this newsroom had access, one of the bodies—brace yourselves—had been severed in half at the abdomen. The intestines and other viscera were removed, and it was clarified that they were not found at the scene. The perpetrators left other body parts scattered in the surrounding area. Another body, belonging to a man of athletic build in his thirties, had a severe skull fracture with exposed brain matter. He also suffered an anal hemorrhage caused by the insertion of a wooden object, as splinters were found in the tissues. The third body had multiple fractures and lacerations, with the eyes gouged out. Like the previously mentioned victim, this one also had a severe anal injury caused by a wooden object. The most bizarre aspect of this case was that all the blood had been drained from the body. The identities of the bodies have been confirmed through fingerprints, and what a surprise the authorities received!

These were not your average law-abiding citizens. They had extensive criminal records—robbery, kidnapping, rape, and extortion. Police suggest that this case bears all the hallmarks of a score-settling between rival drug cartels. Although the brutality was extreme, it is not uncommon among cartels. Here we have photographs of the individuals. The first was known in life as Filiberto Estrada, forty-four years old, originally from Culiacan, Sinaloa. The second was Ignacio Guzman, thirty-two, also from Culiacan. The third was Ramon Fonseca, forty, from Guerrero, Chihuahua. As mentioned, all three had criminal records. They had served as federal ministerial police in Culiacan. Ramon Fonseca held the rank of commander, with the other two under his command. They were dismissed after being accused of torture, rape, and connections to drug cartels on multiple occasions. However, none of the complaints ever prospered. They were eventually transferred to Chihuahua, where they were permanently dismissed after brutally beating some teenagers suspected of robbing a grocery store. The police report also indicates that these men were suspected of leading a gang of home invaders in middle-class neighborhoods, who not only robbed but also raped women and assaulted other family members. The Chihuahua State Police confirmed that several investigations were ongoing against these criminals, but as is customary in our country, nothing could ever be proven. It seems that fate finally caught up with them."

The descriptions of the men and the photographs in the news matched the physiques of the thieves. All the data corresponded. Despite having had their faces covered during the robbery, there was no doubt that it was them. They handled weapons, knew how to neutralize and immobilize people, and used interrogation and intimidation techniques—all skills acquired in police institutions. The modus operandi was identical to what was reported in their criminal history: they had been robbers and were about to rape Fabiola.

"It's them! It's them!" Fabiola exclaimed, her surprise quickly turning into evident emotion.

Braulio couldn't help but smile. Fabiola brought her hands to her mouth, overwhelmed with emotion. They embraced, feeling a slight twinge of guilt for celebrating the torture and death of those men, but it quickly dissipated, replaced by a profound sense of relief and freedom. Why should they feel remorse for the *sons of bitches* who had caused them so much harm, turning the last few days of their lives into a living hell? Not only had they left them nearly bankrupt, but they had also come dangerously close to destroying Fabiola's life and desecrating his uncle Martin's last wishes.

"To hell with them! Let their bodies rot in the depths of hell!" Braulio shouted, clenching his fists in triumph.

They hugged again, kissed, and cried. A torrent of emotions flooded them, but the overwhelming feeling was that of liberation from the terrible psychological prison they had been trapped in.

Once they had calmed down, a flood of questions bombarded them. Should they still report the robbery and attempted rape? Was it wise? What would happen if they didn't? Their first instinct was to say yes, to fulfill their civic duty. However, something made them hesitate. What if the criminals had accomplices within the police force? They remembered the men's boasts about their connections. It was not without reason that they had operated with such impunity for years. It pained them to admit that, in a country like Mexico, where corruption had completely corroded law enforcement, it would be riskier to report a crime—especially if the criminals had shared the secret of their uncle's gold with an accomplice. What if, in filing the complaint and narrating the events, they inadvertently revealed the story of the *Posada del Sol's* centennial gold? The idea of filing a report was quickly discarded. It seemed impossible to recover the stolen items. Perhaps the report would help them negotiate with the banks to collect some insurance and recover part of their money, but it was unlikely, and they would likely spend months, if not years, trapped in a bureaucratic nightmare, dealing with exhausting calls and incompetent, uninterested staff. Not to mention, they would become part of the statistics of millions of Mexicans who do not report crimes for fear of reprisals.

Besides, what did it matter? The criminals had already

received a terrible punishment.

As for telling their family and friends the truth, would it be wise? They agreed it was not. There was always a well-intentioned relative with a loose tongue who could spread the anecdote, eventually reaching the wrong ears. For now, it was better to keep the secret.

It didn't take long before worrying doubts crept into Braulio's mind, somewhat interrupting the joy he felt at his newfound peace. What had happened to the centennials? He remembered the text message in which the thugs had confirmed their findings. Had they managed to extract them? Was it really a score-settling between rival cartels, as the news reported? Why had they been subjected to such violence? Did someone else discover the secret of the gold and decide to eliminate them to claim it? Were the police involved? But none of these doubts caused as much uncertainty in Braulio as Martin's cryptic revelation, left unspoken in the video. Was that the cause of the criminals' deaths? That was an unanswered question that would haunt him for the rest of his life.

CHAPTER 24

A month had passed since they learned of the tragic fate of Ramon, Nacho, and Filiberto. During that time, Braulio and Fabiola tried to normalize their lives. Financially, they were struggling. Their bank accounts were overdrawn, and it would take time to rebuild their savings. The relentless expenses felt like a curse. However, the deepening of their relationship emerged as the one significant gain from all of this. Each day, they enjoyed living together more. Nevertheless, precautions had to be taken after what had happened.

Braulio reinforced the locks on the apartment's main door, subscribed to a burglar alarm installation and monitoring service, and installed a security camera in the hallway. Fabiola reclaimed her old phone number and bought a new cell phone. Judging by her emotional state, it seemed she had returned to normal. She quickly regained the confidence to walk alone through the streets without needing someone by her side. She was a strong woman;

perhaps her training as a lawyer and her experience with difficult cases had toughened her character. Braulio, however, hadn't fully moved past the incident, though he wouldn't admit it. He was on edge, waking at the slightest sound at night, plagued by insomnia. The thought that tormented him during those sleepless nights, buzzing like an annoying mosquito in his ear, was the question of what exactly remained undiscovered. No matter how hard he tried not to dwell on it, the thought seemed to force its way into his mind. It was an undeniably bizarre sensation.

On one of those restless nights, amidst a storm of irrational thoughts, he made a decision that seemed wise: he would see a psychologist to help him rid himself of whatever was disturbing his peace of mind. It was the last vestige of that cursed inheritance from his uncle. He had never looked at it that way before, but since he opened that box, the nightmares had begun, and soon they manifested into reality. It was as if that secret had attracted the thieves. *"With a gift like that, I would've preferred receiving nothing, Uncle,"* he thought, sending a nostalgic yet reproachful message to the afterlife.

After a few days, Braulio's anxiety seemed to have subsided— or at least, that's what he thought until one Tuesday night, when a familiar voice startled him awake. *"Damnatio memoriae,"* the voice whispered.

"Who said that? Was it you, Fabiola?" he asked, startled and sweating.

She, still half-asleep, muttered, "What?"

"I heard a voice, clear as day, saying that phrase: *Damnatio memoriae.*'"

"You must've been dreaming, babe."

"No, I heard it clearly. I think someone broke into the apartment again," he said, his voice tinged with fear.

Fabiola turned on the light.

"Calm down. The alarm would've gone off if someone had. Besides, with those locks you installed, the door could only be broken down by force. We would've heard it."

Braulio jumped out of bed and rushed to the closet, rummaging for something.

"What's that?" Fabiola asked, frowning.

"Is that a gun? Where did you get it, Braulio?" she snapped, her tone laced with concern.

"That's not important. I promised they wouldn't catch us off guard again. This time, I'm prepared."

He grabbed his cell phone to check for alarm alerts but was surprised to find none. He scrolled through another app connected to the security camera, checking the video records, but saw nothing. Fabiola watched him, her annoyance evident.

"Please, Braulio, put that gun away!" she demanded, her voice firm.

Braulio, feeling disoriented, began to calm down. As his mind started to piece things together, he realized it had all been a dream.

"Forgive me; I didn't mean to scare you. I just got nervous. The voice seemed so real, as if someone had whispered it in my ear. I swear."

"Come here, Braulio. But first, put that gun away."

Braulio returned the gun to the closet and then crawled back into bed.

"Where did you get it?" Fabiola asked, her tone carrying a hint of reproach.

"Fabian got it for me. Remember, I told you his brothers are into hunting, and they have weapons? They know how to handle them," he said, shrugging.

"Did you tell him what happened to us?"

"Of course not. I made up a story about some neighbors getting robbed, so I wanted to feel protected."

"Oh, Braulio, I don't like weapons, especially when we don't know how to use them. It unsettles me more knowing you have it. I don't think it's necessary. The security measures we've taken are more than enough. Please, get rid of it, okay?"

Braulio agreed. "You're right. It was foolish of me. I'll return it tomorrow, I promise."

"Do you promise me, Braulio?"

"I'm serious," he said, locking eyes with her.

She hugged him, grateful and comforting him as a mother does a child waking from a nightmare. "Calm down. Try to relax.

Let's go back to sleep. It's almost three in the morning," she said, glancing at the clock. She turned off the light, and they settled back into bed.

"I don't think I'll be able to sleep. These kinds of nightmares always come with insomnia," Braulio said, resigned.

"I think I know a good remedy to help you sleep," Fabiola said playfully, moving closer to him. Braulio soon felt the warmth of her body, her breath, and her sweet, comforting scent.

"And what remedy is that?" he asked, already knowing the answer.

"You'll see..." she whispered in his ear as she kissed him. Soon, their bodies intertwined, and a pleasant fatigue overtook them, lulling them into a deep sleep.

CHAPTER 25

Braulio's day had been anything but good from a work perspective. Problems with customers and suppliers compounded his stress. His boss's unusually high demands and the mounting workload only worsened his situation, draining his concentration. The workday stretched late into the night, and he was the last to leave the office. By the time he stepped outside, darkness had fallen. Overwhelmed, he longed to get to his apartment and rest. Fabiola had mentioned she'd be dining with friends, so he knew he'd be eating alone.

As he arrived at the apartment complex, he noticed the area was darker than usual; several streetlights were out, casting an eerie silence over the place. A chill ran down his spine, and he quickened his pace, anxious to reach the safety of his apartment. An unsettling feeling gripped him, as if he were being watched. The corridors were unlit, amplifying his unease. He lit his way with his cell phone and, upon opening his apartment door, felt frustration bubble up as he realized there was no electricity. It was likely a power outage affecting the whole area. He locked the door securely, set his things down, and began to walk through the apartment. However, the darkness distorted his perception, making the familiar space feel alien. The rooms seemed to close in on him, and the air was thick with the scent of dampness and confinement.

As he continued, he realized he was no longer in his apartment. He now found himself in long corridors that belonged to a place seemingly abandoned. Confused, he turned to retrace his steps, but to his horror, he was standing in the middle of a vast corridor that stretched endlessly in both directions. Cold sweat trickled down his back, and his heart pounded wildly in his chest. He pulled out his phone to call Fabiola, but there was no signal. *"What the hell is going on?"* he muttered under his breath.

The corridor formed a square, with walls about eight feet high. The ceiling and walls bore the marks of time and neglect, with grayish tones and uneven textures. As he shone his light around, shadows danced along the walls, creating the illusion of movement. The place conjured a strange mix of emotions— nostalgia, sadness, despair, and an underlying current of fear. He took cautious steps, trying to make as little noise as possible. At the far end of the corridor, he saw a faint glimmer of light and decided to head towards it. As he moved deeper into the corridor, the oppressive silence was gradually replaced by murmurs and whispers, barely audible but undeniably present. Before long, he thought he heard the distant voice of a child, accompanied by the sound of small footsteps and the rhythmic bouncing of a ball.

"Hello! Is anyone there?" Braulio called out, shivering as the echo of his voice reverberated through the corridor.

"*Damnatio memoriae...* don't let them forget," whispered a tremulous, aged voice, as though someone stood right beside him.

Braulio felt his soul leave his body. That phrase again, but now with additional words. The voice sounded disturbingly familiar. He stood frozen until a young girl's voice broke the silence:

"Is there *kitness* in your heart?" she asked gently.

Braulio turned to his right and saw her. She was a little girl in a white dress, her face a picture of innocence tinged with sadness. Instead of fear, he felt a paternal instinct towards her. He knelt and smiled softly, intuitively understanding what she meant to ask.

"I think you meant the word *kindness*," he corrected, smiling.

The girl nodded shyly.

"Well, I'd like to think so," he replied, still smiling.

The girl took his hand and gestured for him to follow. She seemed to serve as a guide in this desolate place. As they walked, Braulio asked for her name, but she remained silent.

"Are you lost?" he inquired.

"I was," she answered in the carefree tone typical of children.

They continued until they reached a spot where a work lamp lay on the floor, flickering weakly. Its light was dim, barely illuminating the area. Beside the lamp were a pickaxe and some debris. The girl pointed towards a particular spot on the wall. Braulio followed her gesture but saw nothing on its surface. The girl's arm remained outstretched, pointing at something unseen, and she whispered the phrase, *"Damnatio memoriae."*

"What...?" Braulio began, turning back to where the girl had been, only to find that she had vanished.

He spun around, searching for her, but she was gone. He approached the wall, and the lamp's light went out. Using his cell phone as a flashlight, he traced his fingers along the wall's surface and stumbled upon a phrase etched into the stone: *DAMNATIO MEMORIAE*. Intrigued, he ran his fingers over the letters. As he did, a bloody hand shot out from a gap in the wall and grabbed his arm. Braulio recoiled in terror. The hand clamped down on him with a vice-like grip. He struggled to break free, but more hands began to emerge from the wall, which now resembled a massive, blood-soaked wound. Panic seized him as the hands tightened their grip, and desperate, agonized screams echoed through the corridor.

"Free us, for God's sake!" the voices cried out.

"Braulio!... *Mijo!...*" a voice called out, one he immediately recognized in the midst of chaos.

He had no doubt—it was his uncle Martin's voice. Amid the writhing hands, Braulio cried out, "Uncle? Is that you?"

One hand gripped his shoulder while the wall opened wider, revealing his uncle Martin, struggling to break free from the throng of trapped souls. They all fought desperately to escape from within the walls.

"Free me! Free us!" his uncle Martin shouted at him.

The light from Braulio's cell phone caught his uncle's face, ghastly and decomposing, with eyes bulging from their sockets and congealed blood dripping from his nose and mouth. Braulio's terror peaked as he tore himself free from the grasping hands and fell backward. On the ground, he watched as the wall began to crack and crumble. Large chunks of debris rained down on him, striking his face. He shielded himself with his arms as thousands of screams filled the air. He pushed himself away with his legs, watching as his uncle Martin disintegrated into a bloody mass, still pleading for help. Braulio scrambled to his feet and tried to flee down the corridor. But a heavy blow struck him from behind, knocking him to the ground. As everything began to spin, he regained consciousness just in time to see a gigantic figure with a shattered skull raising a pickaxe, ready to deliver a crushing blow. Braulio screamed in terror, powerless to do anything else.

CHAPTER 26

Fabiola was beside him, trying to wake him up.

"Braulio! Braulio! What's happening to you?" she asked, her voice thick with desperation. Braulio opened his eyes, needing a few seconds to realize that he was lying in bed. It had all been a horrible nightmare, the most terrible he'd ever experienced. He was sweating, trembling, his heart pounding wildly. Fabiola held his hand and touched his forehead. He was burning up.

"Easy, babe, you were dreaming. Everything is going to be all right. My gosh, you're boiling; I think you have a fever."

Braulio looked around frantically to ensure he wasn't still trapped in that horrible hallway. Fabiola got up to fetch a glass of water.

"It felt so real, as if I had actually been there," he told Fabiola, recounting every detail of his dream.

"It was just a dream, sweetheart. Try to calm down now," she said, hugging him tightly.

"Tomorrow, you must schedule, without delay, an appointment with the psychologist, as we already discussed. You need help to overcome the trauma we went through and to move past your uncle's death. You can't keep living like this."

Braulio nodded, but deep down, he knew that the solution wasn't a session with the psychologist. The nightmare had convinced him of that. It was the only way he could find peace again.

The next morning, Braulio woke up with a splitting headache, feeling as if he were hungover. He took a cold shower, mulling over what he had to do and how he would do it. He planned to explain everything to Fabiola before leaving for work; he couldn't put it off any longer. Fabiola, wanting to let him rest a bit more, had gotten ready first and was finishing breakfast when Braulio sat down at the table, lost in thought. Fabiola glanced at him and frowned slightly.

"Excuse me for saying this, Braulio, but you look awful. Just look at those dark circles under your eyes. I think I'm going to have to use some of my makeup on you; you can't show up to work like that," she teased, hoping to make him smile.

Braulio remained silent.

"Are you okay?"

"Fabiola, I need to tell you something," he said flatly, his face expressionless.

"What's wrong?" she asked, her concern growing.

"I must go to the *Posada del Sol* to find what I'm convinced is still hidden there—what my uncle couldn't reveal to me. Last night's nightmare was a message. I have to do it."

"What? You've lost your mind, Braulio," Fabiola replied, her expression one of shock.

"I know it sounds crazy, but I'm sure I must do this. All these dreams and nightmares—they're signs. Otherwise, neither my uncle nor I will ever find peace. Please, I need you to understand."

"Do you even realize what you're saying? You're being irrational. If you could hear yourself, you'd understand how crazy it sounds."

"I think I've deciphered the meaning of that phrase, *Damnatio memoriae*. It points to a specific place. It's the notation that was marked on my uncle's blueprints. Do you remember how the second point was labeled '*Oblivion*'? That's what he emphasized so much. I saw it clearly. I could feel it. I still have the sensation in my fingers of the letters engraved on the wall. It's real!"

Fabiola was on the verge of losing her composure entirely. She paced around the kitchen, hands gesticulating in frustration.

"Braulio! Listen, you're not thinking straight," she said, exasperation seeping into her voice.

"Remember the news about the three guys who robbed us and went into the *Posada del Sol* to find your uncle's secret?

146

Remember how they ended up? Don't you realize that place is dangerous? It's cursed. I don't know if its inhabitants are alive or undead, but either way, they're just as dangerous. Please, remember how those gangsters met their end," she finished, her eyes blazing.

"To begin with, we don't know who killed them or why. And we don't even know if their deaths were related to the *Posada del Sol*. You saw their criminal records—they owed a lot to the underworld. It was a reckoning, not necessarily connected to what they were searching for," he concluded with a shrug.

Fabiola pressed both hands to her face, shaking her head, and after a few moments, she said, "Braulio, please reconsider. This is madness. It's far too dangerous."

"I don't have any other choice. I must go. I feel compelled to uncover the secret that haunted my uncle. The dream was a clear message. He's suffering and won't rest until I find it. If you had seen it the way I did…" Braulio's voice trailed off.

"Exactly, you said it yourself—it was just a dream," Fabiola replied, her voice cracking with emotion. She was desperate, overwhelmed by Braulio's stubbornness. Tears of anger and despair began streaming down her cheeks.

"Do you value that damned gold more than your own life… more than our relationship? Don't you understand that you're putting yourself in danger?" Fabiola said, her face flushed with emotion.

147

"I don't care about the centennials. You know that. I'm looking for something else entirely. And what does our relationship have to do with this?"

"Well, if you'd rather throw yourself into the abyss and risk your life instead of seeking professional help to overcome your trauma, I can't follow you into that madness. I'm not willing to lose you. So, I think it's best if we break up. I won't stand by and watch you self-destruct," she said, tears welling up again.

"Babe, please try to understand. I know it sounds crazy, but…" Braulio reached out to hug her, but she pulled away.

"I don't want to hear it anymore! If you don't reconsider, we have nothing else to talk about," she said, heading to the bedroom.

Braulio started to follow her, but he was interrupted by an incoming call on his cell phone. If it had been any other call, he would have ignored it, but the name on the screen left him utterly bewildered. He turned to Fabiola.

"Fabiola, are you calling me?"

"What?"

"Did you accidentally dial my number?"

She turned to face him, her eyes still brimming with tears.

"What are you talking about?"

He showed her the phone. She froze when she saw her name on the screen. She hurried to check her cell phone, which was turned off. When she turned it on and checked her outgoing calls, there were none during that period, much less to Braulio. The call had stopped ringing. A wave of terror washed over them, for that call could only have come from her old cell phone—the one the thieves had taken. They stared at each other, speechless and paralyzed by fear. It didn't make sense. They were more confused than anything else because they reasoned that it was impossible for the criminals to have called.

For one thing, they were dead. But then they thought that maybe the police had found the device and were calling as part of the investigation. However, it was technically impossible since the number had been canceled and reactivated on the new device. What on earth was going on? *They* only called once. A few minutes later, a text message arrived. Sender: "Fabiola." Braulio looked at her, both of them paling. Time seemed to stand still as they silently agreed to open the text message to dispel any doubts. Braulio's heart nearly exploded when he saw the message and the attached file.

"*Damnatio memoriae*... don't let them forget..." he read aloud. The attached photo showed a fragment of a wall inscribed with capital letters: "*DAMNATIO MEMORIAE*."

"It can't be, it can't be," Braulio whispered, all color drained from his face. Those were the only words he could muster. It matched exactly what he had seen in his nightmare.

CHAPTER 27

They sat at the table for a few minutes, staring at the message, trying to make sense of everything. Fabiola was shocked. Braulio felt, for a moment, as if he were in another dream. Everything seemed unreal to him. Could it be a joke? Impossible. They searched for a technological explanation. Perhaps the message had been sent earlier by the thieves and, due to some technical glitch, had been floating in the ether of communication networks, coinciding with the cancellation of the phone number and somehow getting trapped. Sometimes that sort of thing happened. It was one of the explanations they both tried to agree on. It seemed the most plausible, they told themselves, though they soon dismissed it as absurd and fallacious. Neither of them had ever received a text message after so many days. The cold reality hit when Braulio examined the metadata of the message and photo to see what they could reveal about their origin. To his surprise, they were dated January 13, 1982.

They couldn't believe what was happening. That date had no logical explanation. It was an absolute technological impossibility since cell phones, particularly with image messaging, did not exist at the time. Fabiola was stunned, but Braulio was less so because he felt a strange sense of relief. The call and the message only confirmed that he wasn't losing his mind and that the nightmares were messages or cries for help. Braulio knew that the question he was about to ask Fabiola might seem somewhat impertinent, but he needed to ask it.

"Now, do you believe me?"

She looked directly into his eyes, still puzzled. Her expression conveyed disbelief, but deep down, she was beginning to accept that Braulio's nightmares might indeed be messages—or at least, she wanted to believe that. It all still felt like a fantasy to her, a crazy story. But as she began to piece everything together—starting from Martin's initial account, continuing through the ordeal with the damned criminals, their survival, the secret of the *Posada del Sol*, which might have contributed to the criminals' tragic end, Braulio's nightmares, and now the ghostly message—everything seemed connected. There was no way to explain how something seen in dreams was now captured in a digital photograph over forty years old. The paradox, despite everything, seemed the most logical. Now it was Fabiola's turn to ask questions.

"Assuming you go there, do you have any specific plan? How are you going to get into the hotel? Most importantly, how do you intend to find the exact spot in that place if the thieves took the blueprints? From what I remember that place is a labyrinth," Fabiola said, raising her eyebrows.

"Fortunately, I took pictures of the box's contents and digitally scanned the blueprints. I took precautions—not because I suspected theft, but rather for preservation. You know how we engineers are; we have the habit of backing up everything," Braulio answered, shrugging and smiling slightly.

"As for who can help me navigate Mexico City and find a way into the hotel, I've already thought of someone. But I need to ask him in person."

"When do you plan to leave?"

"As soon as possible. The sooner I get this off my back, the better."

"Well, you won't be going alone," Fabiola said firmly.

Braulio was greatly surprised. For a moment, he didn't know what to say.

"I'm going with you," she finally declared.

"Fabiola, it's very dangerous. You said so yourself. I don't want to expose you to any danger. You went through enough with the robbery," he said, holding her hands.

"Well, as I recall, you were more affected by the robbers than I was," she replied playfully.

"Either we go together, or you can forget about this madness."

Braulio was increasingly amazed by the strength of the incredible woman he had as a partner. He was proud and recognized that in many ways, she was stronger than him.

"Okay. Fine," he said with feigned resignation, pulling her into a big hug. He felt lucky to have her support.

CHAPTER 28

They departed on a Thursday night from General Roberto Fierro Villalobos International Airport in Chihuahua, bound for Mexico City. Although Braulio sensed they could be heading straight into the mouth of hell, he felt a surprising sense of relief and peace of mind. Days earlier, he had revealed his plan to Fabiola. He intended to seek out his first cousin, Martin Robledo Jr., who lived in the capital, and tell him everything about his father's secret. Braulio believed it was the right thing to do and should have done it from the start. Martin had a right to know this part of his father's story, no matter how murky and insane it might be. How Martin would react remained uncertain, as he had always expressed a desire to distance himself from anything related to his father due to their turbulent relationship.

Throughout their lives, the two cousins had rarely spent time together, communicating only occasionally through messages and social networks. The last time Braulio had spoken to him was via videoconference, when he offered his condolences for Martin Sr.'s death. The truth was that Martin Jr. had responded very coldly to the gesture.

By revealing his plan, Braulio risked being labeled as crazy or opportunistic. He wasn't seeking to convince Martin of anything or ask him to accompany him to the *Posada del Sol*. He only hoped Martin could connect him with someone who could guide him through the labyrinth that is Mexico City and, in due time, help him gain access to the hotel. Braulio and Fabiola had visited the capital several times for work, not for tourism. And certainly, never to play treasure hunters in haunted hotels. They were unfamiliar with the hotel's surroundings and unsure if it was located in a dangerous area. They knew only that it was situated in the *Doctores* neighborhood, at 139 *Niños Héroes* Avenue.

Braulio had called his cousin in advance, informing him that they would be in Mexico City and that he needed to discuss an important matter with him. He didn't elaborate further. They arranged to meet at Martin's apartment. Initially, Martin had suggested a restaurant as the meeting point, but Braulio mentioned that the subject was too sensitive, preferring a more private setting. Martin then proposed his apartment, intending to prepare a special dish for them, considering it was Friday and that in Mexico City, there is an unwritten rule that after lunchtime, the workday ends, allowing for extended conversations.

Martin Robledo Jr. had taken a path very different from his father's. Four years older than Braulio, he had been married for ten years and had two children: Teresa, nine, and Armando, seven. He had avoided drugs and alcohol all his life. He was an aspiring writer, having independently published a couple of crime novels inspired by his favorite author, the American writer Michael Connelly. Recently, he had secured a contract to publish his next book with a well-known publishing house—a dream come true for him. He planned to release it by the end of the year. To support his family, he worked as a copywriter for an advertising company, earning just enough to get by. His wife, Julieta, two years younger than him, was, like Fabiola, a lawyer, specializing in intellectual property and copyright. Between their two salaries, they maintained a modest middle-class lifestyle.

When they arrived at Martin's apartment, Braulio felt a surge of nervousness. For a moment, he considered turning around and abandoning the whole damn matter. However, he calmed down when Martin greeted them warmly and affectionately. Braulio didn't remember him being so jovial, nor did he expect such a warm reception, considering that Martin had minimal contact with his paternal family and years had passed since they last saw each other in person. Martin bore little physical resemblance to his father, except for some facial features and, most notably, his smile and tone of voice, which were eerily similar. He had a kind demeanor, wore a bushy beard, had light skin, and was of average height. Braulio had always thought he resembled a young Stephen King, except without the glasses. He made a favorable impression on Fabiola. Martin apologized for not being able to introduce them to his wife and children, explaining that Julieta had to attend a meeting to celebrate her law firm's anniversary and that the children were staying with their maternal grandparents. Braulio wasn't bothered by this at all. "I've saved myself the embarrassment of looking ridiculous in front of the whole family when Martin asks me to leave for insulting his intelligence and destroying any last trace of his father's good image," he thought.

Martin had a particular passion for Italian cuisine and had always dreamed of becoming a professional chef. When they arrived, he was in the process of preparing a large bowl of spaghetti *Alla Frutti di Mare*, accompanied by *Livornese* white fish, a dish made with tomato sauce, olives, and basil. The food turned out to be a delight, with pleasant aromas filling the apartment. He served them generous glasses of red wine to accompany the meal.

"So, Braulio, what brings you to Mexico City? What's so important that you had to tell me? Believe it or not, you've left me quite intrigued, especially considering how rarely we see each other," Martin said as they began serving the food.

Braulio cleared his throat, his hands sweating. He didn't even know where to start. He felt nervous, worried about his cousin's reaction. He downed his glass of wine in one gulp. Fabiola took his hand, offering silent support. Martin watched them closely.

"You see, Martin, what I'm about to tell you sounds like something out of a novel," Braulio said, clearing his throat again.

"Even for you, as a writer, it will seem unbelievable. All I ask is that you listen until the end, no matter how uncomfortable some parts might be. The whole story begins with a box your father left me when he died."

"My father?" Martin asked, surprised.

His jovial expression turned stern. Braulio hurriedly poured himself another glass of wine.

CHAPTER 29

Braulio began by describing the contents of the box, recounting everything his uncle had revealed in the video. He was surprised by how vividly he remembered every detail, as though the video played continuously in his mind. This was the third time he had narrated the story, so he had refined every point. He left nothing out. At first, Martin didn't react with disbelief but rather with interest, then surprise. In some parts—especially when Braulio mentioned the corruption of Durazo's accomplices—Martin seemed to unconsciously agree, as if he already knew some of these details. However, when Braulio reached the part about the centennials, Martin's expression became clouded. He brought a hand to his mouth, appearing deeply troubled.

Braulio saved the mention of the mysterious treasure and his absurd request for last. He then described the traumatic encounter with the thieves. His voice wavered slightly, and Fabiola shuddered, recalling how close she had come to being the victim of a brutal assault. Martin was speechless upon hearing how they narrowly escaped, and how fate delivered a bloody end to the criminal trio. Reflecting on the events once more, Braulio was startled to realize how interconnected everything seemed. Perhaps the encounter with the thieves wasn't just a coincidence.

"I'm very sorry, but I'm relieved you made it out of that situation safely," Martin said, his concern genuine.

"In part, it was thanks to your dad's secret. Without it, our fate might have been very different."

Martin nodded, empathetic. He leaned back in his chair, his hands clasped behind his head, staring into space. Braulio and Fabiola exchanged a glance.

"There's something else you need to know," Braulio continued.

Martin gave him a wary look.

Braulio then recounted the cryptic secret and his uncle's request to find the centennials and distribute them among the family. Martin frowned and shook his head.

"Foolish old man," he muttered.

He seemed deep in thought, a flicker of anger crossing his face despite his attempts to conceal it. Braulio paused, anticipating the question that would inevitably follow.

"Why are you telling me all this? Don't tell me you plan to go after the gold centennials," Martin said, raising an eyebrow.

"Not the centennials, but I do intend to recover the *Damnatio*

Memoriae."

"What? I don't understand what you mean," Martin replied, confusion written all over his face.

Braulio explained everything related to the double golden centennial with the Latin inscription. He showed Martin a photograph saved on his phone. That relic, now in the hands of the thugs, confirmed the authenticity of Braulio's story, its golden lure perhaps what kept the criminals at bay. Despite the strained relationship with his father, Martin was familiar with many details and anecdotes of his life. Some were told by his mother, others by relatives or close associates, and many Martin had researched on his own. Perhaps it was this inquisitive nature that had sparked his passion for writing. The irony of his father's involvement in one of the most corrupt police forces in the country always struck him.

Braulio explained that someone had altered the original inscription to engrave the Latin words. Surely, his uncle knew who had done this and why. It was part of what he hadn't been able to explain in the video but was now being revealed to Braulio through dreams—or rather, nightmares. He was convinced they were messages from beyond, as absurd as it sounded. Martin Robledo's soul would not find eternal rest until the mystery behind *Damnatio Memoriae* was unraveled. Braulio knew there was a place where the secret was hidden, and he had seen it clearly.

For a moment, Martin regarded him as though he were

speaking incoherently, as if drunk. But his skepticism faded when Braulio showed him the message and the photograph.

"Do you want to see something completely illogical?" Braulio asked, revealing the metadata.

Martin filled his glass with wine and drank it in a single gulp.

"Wow, I don't know what to make of all this. As you said, it's like something out of a novel. I wouldn't have imagined it," he laughed. "What surprises me most is the phrase in Latin. Do you know what it means?" he asked, his gaze inquisitive.

Fabiola and Braulio nodded.

"*Condemnation of memory*. It means to erase enemies from existence, to wipe them off the face of the earth... What the hell? What does that have to do with...?" He trailed off, lost in thought. He frowned, rubbing his chin. Fabiola and Braulio watched him closely. It seemed he knew something.

Obvious questions followed: How would they uncover the secret? And how would they break through the walls to retrieve it? In response to the first, Braulio showed Martin the digitized blueprints. As for the second, he speculated that the thugs might have already taken care of that part, pointing to the hole visible in the photograph as evidence. The only help Braulio needed from Martin was guidance through the *Doctores* neighborhood to reach the *Posada del Sol*, and assistance in finding someone who could get them inside that ominous place.

They would pose as YouTubers with a passion for horror

legends, their goal to record a video.

To their surprise, Martin was no stranger to the tales of the *Posada del Sol*. He knew its founding history in detail, as well as the craziest legends and ghost stories surrounding it. He joked that their story might soon become part of those legends. However, his expression turned serious and somber when he remarked that the true stories about the hotel could be more terrifying than any legend.

CHAPTER 30

He told them that the *Posada del Sol* became a site for sinister activities after its brief and resounding fall into oblivion. Between the late 1960s and early 1970s, during that terrible period in contemporary Mexico known as the *Dirty War*, the place was used to torture and assassinate left-wing students, dissidents, and political opponents of the old regime. Of course, everything was shrouded in open secrets because, as often happens in Mexico, no formal investigation was ever launched, nor was any public official held directly responsible. Those who dared to speak out were sent into a bureaucratic judicial hell. The disgraced hotel served as the perfect place to operate as an inquisitorial precinct. By a twist of fate, added to the wave of calamities that plagued it since its first stone was laid, it was situated in a strategic area. Just a few meters away were the offices of the corrupt Attorney General's Office of the then Federal District, along with the criminal courts and some headquarters of the feared Federal

Security Directorate. It was even rumored that secret operational cells were established inside the hotel to monitor subversive activities and plan the dissolution of political opposition movements.

There was always a whisper that those arrested and taken to the Attorney General's Office as alleged enemies of the Mexican State, instead of being transferred to criminal courts to face the utopian due process of law, were sentenced in summary trials held at the *Posada del Sol*. Ultimately, all were found guilty, and the sentences were final. According to the accounts of neighbors unfortunate enough to live next to the hotel's perimeter walls, screams and cries could be heard from inside at night. The boldest, who climbed onto their rooftops for a better view of the courtyards, claimed to have seen uniformed police officers pushing, hitting, and cursing naked, handcuffed men with strange hats on their heads, directing them into the hotel's interiors. In those times, unknown individuals were always seen loitering around, like men in suits with dark glasses and grim expressions, guarding the outskirts of the hotel and scaring away anyone who approached to pry.

For a time, it seems, the repressive activities ceased, and the hotel fell into disrepair. Eventually, bureaucratic-administrative offices were established there, remaining until the beginning of López Portillo's six-year term, and *Negro* Durazo came to power as head of the General Directorate of Police and Traffic of the

Federal District. This corrupt figure knew the macabre hotel well, having been an agent of the Federal Security Directorate in the sixties. Thus, the place suited him perfectly as a clandestine headquarters for operations. That's why Martin knew immediately that the centennials' story had to be true. It was said that the corruption in that administration reached insane levels, akin to those seen in Caligula's Rome. They were known to organize bacchanals and orgies in the disgraced hotel, lasting for several days, attended by high-ranking politicians, businesspeople, and artists of the time. The sexual depravity and degeneration that occurred there reached unspeakable levels. There was even talk of Masonic conspiracies and satanic rites performed in the hotel chapel. When exotic celebrations weren't taking place, the government's favorite activities of torture and the disappearance of state enemies continued.

Braulio and Fabiola were shocked by the harshness of the story because, although they had heard some rumors, the level of detail revealed by Martin was overwhelming.

"Braulio, much of the resentment and mistrust I always had towards my father wasn't so much because of his lack of interest and distancing," Martin said with a severe and introspective expression. He cleared his throat a bit. Braulio watched him expectantly, as if waiting for a terrible revelation related to possible family violence.

"It's not what you're imagining. My father never exercised the slightest bit of physical violence against us, despite everything. He always treated my mother like a true gentleman. Looking back, I've concluded that he was sincerely in love with her. My father's problem was that he dwelled in the circles of a Dantesque hell. When I gained the maturity necessary to understand things better, I learned that my father played a significant role in the so-called *Dirty War*. Accurate rumors even reached my ears that he participated in the Tlatelolco massacre, in addition to being a fierce repressor of the supposed enemies of the State. I've writhed in my bed at night, thinking he could have been a participant in the hotel's dark history of torture. It wouldn't surprise me, considering he worked for *Negro* Durazo. No, Braulio, it's hard for me to accept that my father could have become that kind of monster. That's why I never wanted to hear from him, and perhaps, even after his death, I'll never be able to forgive him."

As much as he tried, his voice cracked, and his eyes moistened. Braulio tried to comfort him, placing a hand on his shoulder.

"I can understand your reasons, Martin. However, during all the time I spent with my uncle, I could see deep sadness and regret in him. He lived in constant torture. He always spoke of unspeakable things that devoured his soul and made him dwell in a living hell. When he talked about you and your mother, his soul split in two. I think his punishment was the inability to get close to you. I can assure you that the last years of his life were lived in repentance, and this, like acid, dissolved part of his being until he became the rag of a man he was in the end."

Braulio couldn't help but shed a tear as well. Fabiola snuggled into him and kissed his cheek. Martin hurried to fill the wine glasses, eager to change the subject.

"Cheers!" he said.

The three took a deep drink.

Time had slipped away from them like sand in a desert windstorm. More than three hours had passed, immersed in stories. They discussed some minor details until Braulio, careful not to sound impertinent, tried to steer the conversation back to one of the reasons he had sought out his first cousin in the first place.

"When do you plan to go on your search?"

"Ideally, tomorrow. I want to take advantage of the weekend and finish this as soon as possible."

Martin was thoughtful.

"I already have the ideal person who will not only take you to the *Doctores* neighborhood but will serve as your guide."

Braulio showed some emotion and surprise. He was silent for a few seconds. Fabiola was also watching him expectantly.

"Is it someone you trust? Excuse me for blurting it out like that, but as you may have already noticed, the subject is delicate and tempting," he said, shrugging his shoulders.

"He is someone I trust completely, or at least I think so," Martin said, smiling.

Braulio didn't say anything, but his silence begged to know who his first cousin was talking about. After a while, Martin exclaimed:

"Me."

Braulio and Fabiola were speechless.

"You couldn't find a better person to accompany you. I know the location of the place, and I must confess that a few years ago, in my youth, when I was searching for answers, I entered the *Posada del Sol* with some friends. We wandered here and there, but at the first noise we heard, we ran out like scared chickens," Martin said, laughing.

"Also, like you, Braulio, maybe it will help me find some answers."

"Are you sure? Honestly, I wouldn't want to put you in any dangerous situation."

"Well, I wouldn't want you two to put yourselves in any danger either," he said afterward, smiling.

"It was the same answer I gave him when he told me about his crazy idea of going alone," Fabiola said with a beautiful smile.

"Well, that's settled then. We leave tomorrow, very early."

"What will you tell your wife?"

"The truth. I'm going to take my cousins to see the tourist attractions of Mexico City. Trust me; she'll be glad to get rid of me for a whole Saturday," he said and laughed.

CHAPTER 31

Saturday morning. They arrived early, at a quarter to nine. A heavy, overcast sky loomed over the city, threatening to unleash a torrential downpour. They parked the car a couple of blocks from the place, fortunate to find long-term parking. As they walked along *Avenida Niños Héroes* toward the *Posada del Sol*, the streets bustled with activity despite it being the weekend. Vehicle traffic was moderate. This area of the city was not what Fabiola and Braulio had envisioned. They had imagined the hotel to be in a dangerous neighborhood, the kind often mentioned in the news for rampant assaults and robberies. But to their surprise, the area was large, orderly, perhaps due to the presence of significant government offices.

"There you have the *infamous* hotel," Martin remarked, pointing to a building a few meters ahead.

They were taken aback by what they saw. They had expected something entirely different. The image they had formed in their minds was of a completely desolate place, a building on the brink of collapse, or at best, something resembling the palace of Vlad the Impaler, Prince of Wallachia, surrounded by gargoyles at the corners, with a Gothic facade and signs warning against approaching, complete with barricades of barbed wire.

Instead, they found themselves facing a complex of several buildings, with an eclectic and sometimes inscrutable architecture, displaying veined color tones. They stood on a block that occupied one side of the corner at *Dr. J Navarro Street*, where a five-story building was situated. They observed an extensive wall constructed in two styles: the upper half was composed of black quarry blocks, while the lower half featured beige blocks and limestone. Street artists had decorated them with graffiti, adding an urban touch. From the outside, the hotel did not appear as grand as the one they had seen in the blueprints or videos. The architect had skillfully utilized the space. They were amazed to see that much of the hotel block was filled with stalls selling various products and foods— some offered legal books, others: smoothies and juices, while the ubiquitous delicious tacos with a wide variety of stews, alongside the inevitable traditional Mexican food, were never absent. Some even offered appraisals, plans, and projects. It was reminiscent of a modern-day burg where the hotel served as a fortress and the vendors' stalls as guilds from the old days.

The main facade of the hotel faced *Avenida Niños Héroes*, contrasting with the modern glass building opposite it, which housed the offices of the Superior Court of Justice of Mexico City. The strange facade of quarry blocks consisted of two buildings. On the right side was the first, the largest, with several levels that likely housed the rooms; the left side featured a smaller building with six windows—each one seemingly unrelated to the other, forming semicircles, circles, squares, and ovals. In the middle of them was the entrance gate.

One might have imagined it similar to the entrance of a castle or fortress from a J.J. Tolkien novel. Instead, it was an unremarkable emerald-green gate, rectangular, about twenty meters wide, and three meters high. In the background, a small circular building with several levels was visible. The main entrance was guarded by a kindly-looking man in his sixties, dressed in a security company uniform.

Martin asked Fabiola and Braulio if they wanted to browse the stalls while he spoke with the guard. He approached the man with familiarity, explaining that he was a filmmaker scouting locations for an upcoming movie and even making a false promise to cast him as an extra. He added that his scriptwriter and cinematographer were accompanying him. The guard watched them with some skepticism but couldn't help smiling, as he often heard such stories. To seal the deal, Martin slipped him a couple of crisp bills.

"Don't tell me you're bringing in construction tools and equipment. If so, you better get the hell out of here. I'm not letting you in. Some shady-looking guys came by a while ago, and I never saw them leave—at least, not during my shift."

He asked Martin to wait about ten minutes while he made the necessary arrangements and then instructed them to enter discreetly, as if they were simply going about their business. Martin took the opportunity to visit one of the stalls and returned with a large bag, which he stuffed into the small backpack he was carrying.

"What's that?" Braulio asked.

"For the *tribute*," Martin replied.

CHAPTER 32

The cloudy weather cast a different hue over the building. Inside, the atmosphere became cooler. The bustle of the street faded into a pleasant silence, complemented by the soothing smell of rain and wet earth. It was incredibly calm, almost monastic. Martin led the way, assuming the role of a tour guide. Fabiola and Braulio were captivated by the place. Despite the eccentricity of the architecture, which some had described as schizophrenic, it was not in poor taste. Instead, it formed a unique style they had never encountered before. Soon, they entered what had once been the hotel's main hall.

The architectural amalgamation was impressive, merging various styles into a cohesive whole. The design ranged from Roman-style columns and arabesque details, with hints of Hindu influence, to Mesoamerican elements. Martin explained that much of the material used in the construction and artisanal decoration included tezontle, marble, volcanic rock, and meticulously stylized Talavera tiles. As they advanced through the opulent interior, they encountered railings and ironwork shaped into surreal designs. The floor was adorned with large tiles that resembled a chessboard. Next, they passed by a massive arch-shaped chimney built with brick and quarry stone, adorned at the top with motifs resembling leaves and fruits, each corner ending with a lion's face. At the top, an inscription was engraved in stone: "*Fire. You are friend and executioner. You are tea and scourge. You are sun and death. You are star and crater. Fire. As man's elder brother, accompany him on his path to happiness and eternal progress.*"

Fabiola and Braulio took photos and videos of everything. Fabiola couldn't help but feel a pang of sorrow for the neglect and abandonment that plagued the place. They moved on to an open-air corridor leading to a patio where two enormous pink stone arches stood, their edges adorned with Talavera details. These arches framed a vibrant mural narrating a chapter in Mexican history: the promulgation of the *Apatzingán* Constitution, the first step toward Mexican independence. The mural featured José María Morelos y Pavón and other significant figures of that historical moment. Braulio thought this was an excellent place to analyze the blueprints and locate the corridors that housed the centennials and the other secret.

He had printed a copy of the digitized document. As they watched, distant lightning rumbled. After a few minutes, they determined the course they should follow. Fabiola, enchanted by the picturesque surroundings, expressed disbelief that the hotel could be cursed, let alone that such heinous acts as those they had reviewed the day before could have been committed there.

"It's a place of appearances, Fabiola, much like we humans sometimes are. The most angelic-looking person you encounter might harbor a terrible demon within," Martin observed.

They decided to continue. In the central courtyard, they came across a vast Olmec stone head. Its presence here was disconcerting; it appeared to be an original piece. They passed by a post with a bell attached. The hair on their arms stood on end as Martin reminded them of the legend about the hotel's founder, who supposedly took his own life by hanging himself from that very post.

"This place harbors many secrets and legends, as well as some rather intriguing attractions, such as the existence of a theater within."

Fabiola and Braulio looked at him skeptically.

"But that will be the subject of another visit, should we return," he said with a smile.

"We're getting closer to the entrance of the corridors," Braulio noted as he examined the plans.

"What follows is something that has always unsettled me," Martin warned.

They stopped in front of a quarry inscription with decorative mosaic details located near the exit of the hotel chapel. It was more of a testament, mixing grievances with a slight warning to those who, in one way or another, had hindered the majestic project of the architect and founder, Fernando Saldaña Galván: "I only recommend to anyone who pleases, those vain and aggrandized individuals without their own merits, who tried to humiliate me and burdened me with difficulties or climbed over me to increase their grandeur and heritage, while I worked relentlessly and without hope. Time will speak *suum cuique*, citizens of the world respect for work is the purpose of every revolution. FSG February 22, 1945."

Fabiola felt a slight tremor in her heart. Sadness lingered over that inscription.

Braulio was unnerved by the stone statues near the chapel's entrance. One depicted a monk, accompanied by a menacing-looking dog. Martin informed them that it was Saint Francis of Assisi and the Gubbio wolf. According to legend, in ancient times, the ferocious beast terrorized the city of Gubbio in Italy, devouring animals and people alike. No one could stop it until Saint Francis, moved by his compassion for the city's inhabitants, intervened, risking his own life to tame the wolf with a sign of the cross. From then on, the wolf never attacked the city again.

They walked to the simple wooden door that led to the small, circular chapel. They pushed it, but it was locked. They had seen videos and photographs revealing that its architecture was as enigmatic as the rest of the site. The legends surrounding the chapel were also disconcerting, speaking of all kinds of rites and even human sacrifices. Others claimed it was an initiation site for secret lodges.

"The entrance is at the end of this corridor," Braulio said while studying the blueprints.

They walked down the corridor. Further on, they encountered some steps, which they descended. It was a passageway with volcanic stone walls, as if foreshadowing the darkness ahead. As they walked, the statue of Saint Francis and the wolf seemed to be watching them. It was an eerie feeling.

At the end of the corridor, they came to a rusty metal door, slightly ajar. Braulio pushed it cautiously. It emitted a discreet creak, accompanied by a loud clap of thunder from the sky. The storm was imminent. They jumped, and Fabiola clung to Braulio.

"We still have time to turn back," Martin cautioned.

Braulio looked at Fabiola. She gently squeezed his hand in support.

"Let's finish this, once and for all."

A dark corridor lay before them. Before entering, Braulio and Martin took out flashlights from their backpacks. They also had bottles of water, portable phone chargers, and small mallets, just in case.

CHAPTER 33

As soon as they took the first step into the corridor, they felt a slight drop in temperature. Fabiola wrapped herself in a shawl she had thrown into her backpack and took Braulio by the hand. The space was vast and dark, illuminated only by the faint light filtering through small, elongated windows high on the left wall. An awkward silence filled the air. They couldn't help but think of those horror movies set in abandoned psychiatric complexes. Martin moved cautiously, his attention caught by strange inscriptions and drawings on one of the dilapidated, faded walls. The images, which resembled improvised graffiti, had been drawn with chalk. One looked like a character from a children's cartoon about insects, seemingly greeting the visitors. Beside it was a colored star with an eight-pointed geometric shape and a darker, horned figure. Underneath, incoherent phrases were scrawled: *"The night that doesn't come will come," "Ephemeral Ballesteros pass,"* and *"Plains of turtledoves ahead."*

"What kind of twisted mind thought this was a suitable place for artistic expression?" Martin wondered, feeling a slight chill. During his previous visit to the hotel, he hadn't ventured as deeply into its bowels as he was now. He had an odd sensation he couldn't quite explain. The peculiar charm of the hotel had been replaced by a funereal atmosphere.

"What a strange place... These corridors weren't meant to be rooms. Maybe they were intended as storage or machine rooms," Braulio whispered.

"Or perhaps for torture and murder," Martin replied sarcastically.

Both felt chills. They paused for a moment while Braulio consulted the blueprints. His engineering training allowed him to quickly read and interpret the documents, and he indicated where they needed to go.

They reached a door that was barely hanging on its hinges, seemingly superimposed. They pushed it open cautiously, its rusty hinges groaning softly. They entered a small, pitch-black room. Braulio shined his flashlight toward a corner where something was piled up in the gloom. The sight made Fabiola stifle a scream.

"It's the altar of the girl I told you about, the one you saw on YouTube," Martin said.

Fabiola and Braulio approached cautiously, eyeing the scene with suspicion. The first thing that caught their attention was a purple rubber ball with eyes and a mouth painted on it, its expression insane. It sat on a makeshift wooden table against the wall, surrounded by an assortment of sweets. Above the table hung an old, discolored dress, withered by time. Leaning against the left side of the table was a portrait of a little girl dressed in white, apparently from her first communion. She wore a headband resembling rabbit ears, and beside her were several small vases. Fabiola couldn't help but feel sadness for the girl's fate, as hinted by the anecdotes. Tragic stories involving children always disturbed her.

As Braulio looked at the portrait, he felt a chilling tingle creeping up his body. The girl was the same one who had held his hand in his dream, her expression frozen. He turned pale. Martin placed a hand on his shoulder.

"Are you all right, Braulio?" he asked.

"Babe, are you okay?" Fabiola added quickly.

"She's the same girl I saw in my dreams. The one I told you about."

Martin and Fabiola exchanged uneasy glances, unsure of what to say.

"We'd better keep moving and finish as quickly as possible. Let's go," Braulio said, taking Fabiola's hand to continue.

"Wait!" Martin interjected.

"What's going on?"

"We need to leave a tribute for the girl at the altar," Martin replied, pulling out a plastic bag filled with sweets and chocolates from his backpack.

"Each of you take a handful and place it on the table, wishing her pleasure and enjoyment." They did as he instructed, arranging the offerings on the improvised altar. Braulio felt a shudder in his soul as he placed a chocolate bar on the table, wondering why he felt such unease.

Braulio signaled them to proceed toward a door on the side of the room. According to the blueprints, it led to a series of intricate corridors that would take them to their objective. As they advanced, the atmosphere grew increasingly gloomy. Feelings of nostalgia and sadness began to overwhelm them, and unpleasant, long-buried memories started to surface—voices of the soul. But what worried them most was the growing sense that they were being watched, as if someone was following them. Martin mentioned hearing footsteps.

"The desolation of this place is starting to mess with our minds," he whispered.

They both nodded in agreement. Fabiola clung tightly to Braulio's arm. The corridors became disorienting, distorting their sense of time. It felt as though they had been wandering for weeks, yet when Fabiola checked the clock on her phone, only twenty minutes had passed. Braulio and Martin continued to illuminate the path ahead as they navigated through the darkness, halting when they encountered debris on the ground.

"This must be the entrance marked on the blueprints," Braulio said, shining his flashlight on a massive hole in one of the corridor walls.

They checked the blueprints to confirm. Braulio's heart began to race as he realized that this entrance had been created by the trio of criminals. The thought of encountering them inside made him hesitate, which Fabiola noticed.

"Honey, there's nothing to worry about. Remember, they're dead; we saw it on the news. And they haven't bothered us since," she reassured him.

"You're right," Braulio agreed.

Martin watched them nervously, his eyes wide with anxiety. The three of them stared down a narrow, elongated, and macabre corridor that seemed endless. Braulio estimated the space to be about eight feet tall and wide. Martin noted the stark contrast between the finishes of the walls and ceilings here and those in the areas they had just visited.

"It's as if sinister and corrupt hands have used them as canvases to depict their depravity," he muttered.

CHAPTER 34

The atmosphere thickened further. They attempted to speak softly, as the echo created a strange distortion in their voices. They moved cautiously, as if trying to avoid waking the dead. Fabiola mentioned she felt as though they were inside a vast mausoleum—a sentiment everyone shared. No better description could be found. As they ventured deeper, a sense of a presence crept upon them. It felt as though a fourth figure had joined their group. They illuminated the entrance but saw no one. Deciding to quicken their pace, they hoped to escape that insidious place as soon as possible.

Braulio noted that, according to the map, they were only a few meters from the spot where the gold centennials were supposedly hidden. As they advanced, Braulio stumbled over something bulky. He bent down to examine it, shocked to discover it was the hinged double centennial his uncle had left him, the one stolen from Braulio on that fateful night. He showed it to Martin, who inspected it and read the Latin phrase. Martin appeared both thoughtful and puzzled as he returned it to Braulio. They continued onward, but soon noticed a strange reflection on the ground from their lanterns.

"My goodness!" Martin exclaimed.

Scattered across the floor were several gold centennials. Martin picked one up, admiring the shiny, beautiful head of the coin. The image depicted the angel of independence holding a laurel wreath in his right hand, while broken chains hung from his left. Turning the coin over, he saw an old national coat of arms, but his expression twisted with revulsion when he noticed the eagle was smeared with a dark substance. He knew what it was. He threw the coin to the ground.

"This is *bloody* gold," he warned.

Braulio and Fabiola were startled, not just by this revelation, but by what they encountered next.

Less than a meter ahead, the floor was covered with large chunks of rubble—bricks, stone, cement, and dust. They shone their lights, revealing a work lamp on the ground beside a gaping hole in the wall. It resembled the entrance to a dungeon. Their hearts pounded in their chests, not from anticipation, but from sheer uncertainty. Fabiola covered her mouth to stifle a rising cry. Braulio looked at her in surprise. She was staring at the floor, horrified by what she saw—a vast, grotesque scab of blood adorned with what seemed to be human remains. It was the grim evidence of Filiberto's execution.

"I think it would be best to leave this place immediately," Martin urged in a strained voice. Braulio was about to agree when something stopped him.

"*Damnatio memoriae*," whispered a faint voice that belonged to none of them.

They froze, and it was then that Braulio realized he had to press on and make a decision.

"I have to continue, Fabiola. You should wait for me at the entrance. I've already exposed you to enough danger."

Fabiola shook her head.

"What are you talking about? I'm not leaving you here alone!"

"You won't be leaving me alone. You'll be waiting at the entrance," he insisted, turning to Martin. "I'm asking a huge favor. Please, go with her. Stay safe, both of you. I must go on. It's not fair to put you both in harm's way."

Martin considered for a moment. He looked at Fabiola, and almost in unison, they responded.

"No way. We've come this far. We're family, and we must protect each other. I heard that voice too. Something tells me we need to keep going," Martin said firmly.

Fabiola nodded.

"We're all in this together, and we won't leave you behind."

Braulio didn't fully agree, but a part of him was relieved. The thought of being left alone was unbearable.

"Then let's hurry." Forget those damn centennials. As you said, it's bloody gold," Braulio said, checking the blueprints. "The spot we're looking for is about ten meters ahead."

They quickened their pace, but it was difficult to ignore the oppressive atmosphere surrounding them. Strange murmurs filled the air, and the sound of footsteps behind them grew louder. Rushing voices overwhelmed their minds, as if they were pushing through a dense brush that obstructed their path. Something urged them to stay strong and ignore everything to reach their destination. Braulio held Fabiola's hand tightly as she illuminated the encroaching darkness. Martin's face was etched with anguish and anxiety, but a familiar voice managed to calm and encourage him. He had never experienced anything like this before. Suddenly, Braulio recognized the location. It matched the place he had seen in his dreams and in the ghostly photograph they received.

They came across another work lamp lying on the floor, its light flickering as it died. Next to the lamp was a pickaxe amid the debris. Braulio knew where to direct the light.

The words engraved on the wall appeared: "*DAMNATIO MEMORIAE.*" His chest tightened as if it were about to explode. Above the Latin phrase was a huge hole, and beside it, another large black stain, as if paint had been splattered on the wall. He suspected what it was but chose to ignore it.

"This is it. What we're looking for is inside the wall."

Fabiola and Martin watched anxiously. In the distance, they heard a noise and shone their lights, glimpsing a shadow moving swiftly. Fear gripped them, but they maintained their composure. Succumbing to panic would spell doom in a place like this.

"What should we do?" Martin asked.

Despite the large hole in the wall, Braulio realized it wasn't big enough to squeeze through. The answer was clear. He picked up the nearby pickaxe and decided to continue the work that had been left unfinished. The noise worried him, but at this point, what did it matter? He looked at Fabiola and Martin for confirmation. They both nodded. Then he struck the wall. The sound was terrifying, as if the wall itself were alive. Something urged him to keep going. Soon, exhaustion set in, and his hands ached. Martin offered to take over. When he delivered the first blow, he nearly fell backward from the shock. It felt like a groan emanated from deep within. He hesitated, unsure if he should continue. "Go on!" an inner voice urged. As he struck again, he heard a ghostly voice: "*Damnatio memoriae… don't let them forget…*"

A surge of adrenaline pushed him to deliver one final blow that shattered the wall, revealing a large entrance as the last piece of brick fell. They couldn't yet see what lay beyond.

The dust created a haze, causing them to cough as they wiped away sweat. As the dust settled, they took the opportunity to drink some water and pause briefly. They illuminated the collapsed wall and saw that it was double-layered.

The interior space was narrow, barely two feet wide. Braulio was the first to enter. The smell was rancid, putrid. He donned a face mask. The stench was unbearable. Less than a meter away, he found what he had been searching for.

CHAPTER 35

It was a large, black-painted aluminum box. Time had oxidized it, giving it a strange hue. It resembled a trunk or a small chest. Braulio asked Martin for help to drag it out. They observed it with caution. What could be hidden inside that godforsaken box that had caused Martin Robledo such sorrow, turning it into an obsession that transcended death? They were about to find out. Braulio couldn't endure the uncertainty any longer. They decided to open it, only to discover that the main latch was secured with a strong padlock. They tried to force it open, but it was useless. They would have to break it. Martin took the initiative, and Braulio asked him to be careful not to damage the contents inside. After a few hits with the pickaxe, the padlock finally gave way. They hadn't noticed that the murmurs and voices that had been afflicting them had gone silent for some time. It was as if they were waiting. A sense of calm settled in the atmosphere, yet their nerves were on edge. What if some hellish force emerged when they opened it and annihilated them, like in a classic horror movie? But they soon realized that the regret of not doing so would consume them more brutally. They positioned themselves to open it.

"This belongs to you, Braulio," Martin said.

Fabiola nodded. Braulio placed both hands on the top of the lid and pushed it back. The contents were finally revealed.

Inside were black, hard-cover record books, stacked in two rows, fitting almost perfectly into the box. Some were labeled with white stickers bearing the acronym "FDS," followed by successive numbers starting from 667. Another set of books had dark green hard covers and was identified with the acronym "GDPT"; in this case, the successive numbering started from 45. The passage of time had left its mark on them. Before skimming through the contents, they counted the books—seven with the initials "FDS" and five with "GDPT." Braulio handed one to Martin, and Fabiola illuminated them with the flashlight. Braulio opened the first book and saw that its pages were filled, according to a format, with lists of people's names, starting with paternal and maternal surnames, first names, ages, physical complexions, last known addresses, dates of arrest, and the criminal or subversive groups to which they were allegedly affiliated. The book Martin was examining, one labeled "FDS," contained the same registration data, with only a few minor variations. His expression was one of disgust, and as he turned each page, his face contorted more and more. He was speechless.

"I can't believe it," he whispered.

Braulio watched him closely.

It was clear that these were police records, and Braulio noticed that all the records corresponded to male names. But something else in Martin's expression revealed that he had realized something he hadn't yet shared with them.

"What's going on, Martin? Do you know what this is all about?"

"I think I can imagine," Martin replied in a dull tone, without taking his eyes off the book. His heart was pounding, and he was sweating profusely.

"And?" Braulio asked, his impatience growing.

Martin looked up and met Braulio's gaze.

"These are police records from the former Federal Directorate of Security and the city's General Directorate of Police and Traffic. These acronyms represent their respective initials. The records date from the late sixties to the year eighty-two of the last century," Martin said, pausing with a broken voice, as if on the verge of tears. "From the way the descriptions are written, I'm convinced that..." He cleared his throat.

He struggled to get the words out. Fabiola and Braulio watched him with a mix of uncertainty and dread, sensing what Martin already knew.

"I'm convinced this is the list of the disappeared victims of the *Dirty War* perpetrated by the government of that time."

If true, the revelation was devastating. They froze, confused and breathless. Initially, they couldn't grasp the magnitude and implications of the discovery. But gradually, they began to understand. It represented a historical event and justice for all the victims' relatives, who had lived in a brutal hell of uncertainty for decades, not knowing the fate of their loved ones who had been taken by a ruthless, intolerant, and repressive regime. There is no worse earthly hell. The implications for the government would be shocking, even though these were events of the past. It was a nuclear bomb. Politicians would line up to exploit it, as always, using firewood from the fallen tree to gain some votes. They soon realized that the books only represented part of the puzzle—they still had to find out where the bodies were.

The answer came in the form of a small note that slipped from one of the pages of the book Braulio was holding. It contained a detail that shouted back at them. It was an old requisition for the purchase of cement bags and bricks. On the back was a brutal and demonic phrase: *immurement material.*

Braulio threw the book away in revulsion, and Fabiola groaned in horror. Martin turned pale again. They turned toward the long wall. They felt it—they knew it. The voices and murmurs were back. There they were. It was as if the pleading, terrified screams had been analogically recorded on the walls. They had been buried alive. They had been immured in those damn walls like in the Middle Ages. Immurement was a brutal torture that involved placing the condemned in an extremely narrow space and enclosing them inside a wall covered with bricks and cement, as evidenced by the walls of those nefarious corridors. Death was slow; it could take days or even weeks before the person died of dehydration or starvation. Terrible and monstrous, there was no other way to describe it.

They could almost hear the voices crying out for justice, wanting to be released and given eternal rest. There, they understood the meaning of the Latin phrase *Damnatio memoriae*. Those infernal beings, the repressive arms of the government, had applied the "condemnation of memory" to all those people in its literal sense, just as the Romans had done. They condemned the memory of an enemy of the state after his death, erasing it completely to hide a state crime.

Braulio had finally obtained the missing piece that his uncle, Martin Robledo, had left him in the video—erased as part of a curse to perpetuate the memory's condemnation. It was clear. He saw it in images. When his uncle Martin had been in that same place more than forty years ago and they had opened walls to hide the centennials, he would have discovered the immurement and what was hidden there—something that, according to Martin himself in the video, was confessed by one of its perpetrators, horrifying him. It was he who left the clue with that Latin phrase.

It couldn't be that obvious. He used a phrase that any corrupt policeman or politician would struggle to decipher. *Never to forget*, as a constant reminder, it was Martin who marked the gold centennial of Durazo. Braulio realized that his uncle had not participated in such brutal events because, as he had told him in the video, it was during his time there that he learned about the terrifying torture, something that haunted him for the rest of his days.

"Your father didn't stain his hands with blood in those events, Martin," Braulio said with some emotion as he explained the details.

Martin was deep in thought. In a way, knowing that felt like a massive weight had been lifted from him.

They decided to get out of that damned place as soon as possible. They had to take those records and reverse the condemnation of memory—make it known to the world. They hurriedly put the books away and closed the box.

"Let's go," they said hastily.

"You're not going anywhere, you bastards!" came a threatening voice from behind them.

CHAPTER 36

It wasn't a ghost. *The living are more to be feared than the dead.* In the brief moment they managed to glimpse him in the light of their flashlights before he ordered them to drop them on the floor, they saw a man dressed in black. He was of medium height, with a robust build, shaggy hair, coarse features, and a sparse mustache. He pointed a Beretta 380 pistol at them while dazzling them with a flashlight in his other hand, ordering them to keep their hands where he could see them.

"I knew you were the sons of bitches who killed my brother and his friends to rob them," he growled in a thick *Sinaloan* accent, his bloodshot eyes glaring.

They were paralyzed, utterly shocked. It was difficult to determine if it was the presence of the living or a ghostly apparition.

"What brother? What are you talking about?" Braulio asked hesitantly.

"Don't play dumb with me, you prick," he snarled, aiming the gun more firmly at him.

"My brother, Filiberto, told me some asshole from Chihuahua City had given them a map to a hidden treasure in this hotel and that they would come looking for it. Hundreds of gold coins, he said. At first, I didn't believe him because, even though I loved my brother, he was a fucking drug addict who spent his time talking and doing all sorts of stupid bullshit. But when I heard on the news that they were found dead in a drain, horribly tortured, I knew the story was true. Too many coincidences. I immediately put the pieces together and knew it was related."

Braulio realized he was talking about one of the thieves who had broken into his apartment. He turned to Fabiola, who also understood. Fear began to creep over them. Braulio couldn't find the words to respond. Fabiola started to sob. Martin stood by, expectant.

"You know who I mean, right, asshole?" the man taunted. They remained frozen.

"So, I started to investigate. The only clue I had was that a treasure was hidden among some secret corridors at the *Posada del Sol* hotel. My brother didn't tell me anything else. I took the initiative to come here, to Mexico City, *Chilangoland*, and watched all the idiots who entered the hotel. I followed them to see if they knew the secret location. But they were all just a bunch of assholes, sniffing around, looking for ghosts, getting high, and finding places to have sex. I spent days and weeks like that until you guys showed up. I followed you and was shocked to see that you went in another direction. And well, here we are. The bastards guided me to the gold," he said, laughing mockingly and waving his arms.

Martin seized the brief distraction to try disarming the man, but he was quicker. After a brief struggle, Martin ended up receiving a solid blow to the forehead from the butt of the pistol. He collapsed to the ground as blood began to gush from his head. Dazed, he whimpered in pain. The man kicked him in the stomach and aimed his gun at him. Fabiola clung to Braulio.

"You fuckers better calm the fuck down. Another attempt to play hero, and you're dead," he barked in a menacing voice.

"In any case, what happened to my brother will not go unpunished. No way. I will do the same thing to you sons of bitches that you did to him. You can't imagine what I have in store for you. But first, you're going to help me get the treasure out of here," he said with an almost maniacal grin.

"Get up, you bastard!" he ordered Martin. Braulio helped him to his feet, Martin's face drenched in blood, feeling dizzy.

"What do we have here?" the man muttered as he approached the chest. He ordered Braulio to open it. When he saw the contents, he frowned.

"What the hell is this? Where's the gold? My brother spoke of solid, government-issued gold coins."

"The centennials are over by the wall," Braulio replied.

The man hesitated, frowning.

"Then start walking. Take that box with you—it must have some value," he ordered, gesturing with the gun.

As they reached the spot where the entrance to the double wall hiding the centennials were located, the man saw the enormous scab of blood scattered on the floor, and fury twisted his face.

"You motherfuckers! This is where they were killed!" he screamed, delivering a brutal punch to Braulio's stomach. Braulio doubled over, leaning against the wall, struggling to breathe. Fabiola was terrified. Martin was still reeling from the blow to his head.

The man crouched and picked up several gold coins from the floor, examining them as a wide smile spread across his face.

"So, it's true. Where's the rest?"

"Inside," Fabiola replied.

Braulio was still gasping for air. Martin was using his sleeve to wipe away the blood. Fortunately, his wound had stopped bleeding.

"Here's what we're going to do. You two assholes will go into that hole and bring out all the coins. I'll wait here with this doll," he said, leering at Fabiola.

"And if you try anything smart again, she'll be the first one I shoot. Once you gather everything, we'll walk out of this place like fans of horror stories. We'll load everything into my vehicle, and if you behave well, play by the book, maybe I won't make you suffer too much," he added sarcastically.

Braulio and Martin entered what looked like a catacomb at first glance. It was narrow, and the stench of confinement was overwhelming. They made their way with a flashlight the man had handed them. Martin was still dizzy, leaning on Braulio for support. A few meters ahead, they saw a black shape. It turned out to be a giant bag made of a thick nylon-like material. The zipper was slightly open, revealing hundreds of gold centennials inside. Their jaws dropped as Braulio thrust his hand into the coins, feeling them like grains of wheat in a sack.

Outside, the man kept his gun trained on Fabiola, who was leaning against one corner of the enormous hole. He didn't take his eyes off her, his gaze full of lust. She felt deeply uncomfortable.

"Maybe I'll spare your life, precious," he said.

Fabiola glared at him with contempt.

Suddenly, the man felt something land right at his feet. He looked down and shone the flashlight on it. To his shock, it was a purple rubber ball with a strange face that seemed to be staring at him.

"What the hell...?"

"Everything okay, little friend?" a strange voice asked behind him.

He spun around, startled. There stood a uniformed policeman, wearing a jacket, a black tie, and shoulder patches of faded yellow. A badge was pinned to the left side of his coat. The man aimed his flashlight at him but lowered his gun when he realized who it was. He reached into his right pants pocket and pulled out a badge, showing it to the officer.

"Federal Public Ministry. I'm Agent Estrada, investigating a homicide of federal agents that allegedly took place here. I'm guarding the suspects. I'm in charge here, officer. We don't need local police, so you can go," he said arrogantly.

The policeman laughed—a sound that echoed like hundreds of voices layered on top of each other.

"That badge has no value here. In this place, you are nothing! Filthy human scum," he spat, his voice almost guttural.

Fabiola watched from her corner, horrified as she finally made out the policeman's face. She froze.

"You're seconds away from being nothing either, you fuck!" Agent Estrada shouted, cocking his gun and firing a burst of shots at the policeman. A cacophony of laughter echoed off the walls, creating an eerie sound effect.

Braulio and Martin heard the gunfire from inside. Panic seized Braulio as he desperately shouted, "Fabiola! Fabiola!" while running back. Martin followed close behind. Emerging from the wall, they saw six uniformed men. Two of them had subdued the man who had identified himself as Agent Estrada. He screamed desperately, "Let go of me, you bastards!"

Relief washed over them at the sight. Fabiola flung herself into Braulio's arms. Martin stared at the uniformed men, terror in his eyes.

"We're safe," Braulio said to Martin, trying to reassure him that everything would be alright.

Martin turned to him, his eyes wide with fear.

"Braulio, those are uniforms from the city's General Directorate of Police and Traffic."

"So?"

"They're over forty years old!"

As he finished speaking, they watched in horror as the policeman wearing the highest-ranking uniform delivered a brutal blow to Agent Estrada's head with a wooden stick. He fell like a sack of potatoes. The uniformed men then turned their gaze to Fabiola, Braulio, and Martin. The light from their flashlights illuminated their faces, and what they saw shook them to their core. Those faces. They tried to run but were soon surrounded by four human figures dressed in strange black robes. Yellow and red lines formed intricate designs on their chests. They wore pointy hoods over their heads. Never had they felt such fear. The figures surrounded them, and the last thing they perceived was an enormous veil falling over them, leaving them in a comforting daze.

CHAPTER 37

Braulio was the first to open his eyes, lying on his back, feeling an overwhelming lethargy. He initially believed that the celestial dome above was part of his dream, but reality soon asserted itself. The structure overhead resembled a church dome, with an ornate lamp hanging from the center, its intricate details dimly illuminated by flickering candlelight. The dome had two levels, encircled by a wooden railing, with frescoed landscapes and small oval windows of translucent marble guarded by owl figurines. The tranquility of the place was almost suffocating.

Braulio attempted to stand but found his hands and feet bound. He struggled desperately, but it was futile. Turning his head, he saw Fabiola, Martin, and Agent Estrada in the same predicament. They were lying on something resembling altars arranged in a circle. Braulio called out to Fabiola, who began to wake up, groggy as though drugged.

"Fabiola! Are you okay?"

"Braulio? What's happening? Where are we?" she exclaimed, her voice trembling as she realized her restraints. Panic surged through her, and she started screaming, thrashing against the bonds.

"Calm down, Fabiola!"

"What's happening? What's happening?" she cried in despair.

"Braulio!" Martin's voice came from the other end.

They could barely see each other.

"Here I am!" Braulio responded.

"I think we're inside the hotel chapel," Martin said, his voice heavy with concern. A chill ran down Braulio's spine.

Agent Estrada began to regain consciousness, but the brutal blow he had received left him disoriented. The left side of his face was mangled, and he could only utter incoherent sounds.

Out of nowhere, whispers began to fill the air. Behind the main altar—a vertical rectangle of veined marble blocks in shades of brown, with a vast hollow cross—four hooded figures appeared. They positioned themselves around the captives, standing at each interior flank. Their ghastly arms crossed, their hollow gazes fixed on their prisoners, instilling paralyzing fear.

A man in a police uniform suddenly emerged. None of them had sensed his approach. He was the same one Agent Estrada had encountered earlier. His face was unreadable, his features indistinct, his gaze piercing and contemptuous. His grimaces exuded arrogance. Fabiola couldn't stop crying, and Braulio was struck silent, unable to form a coherent thought. Only Martin managed to speak: "Who are you?"

The question hung in the air until a distant voice replied.

"We are the concentration and residue of all the evil and human rot out there; we feed on the vileness, envy, corruption, and betrayal of double-faced people. Our circle comprises politicians, drug dealers, rapists, murderers, kidnappers, and pedophiles. The worst of the worst. We are eternal." The voice was otherworldly, composed of thousands of overlapping tones.

The answer froze them in place. The uniformed man began to walk around the circumference, clearly aiming to intimidate them, whipping a pointed stick over his left hand. The hooded figures started chanting in a strange language. A sharp dagger appeared in their skeletal hands. Tears welled in Braulio's eyes as he sensed the end was near.

"Let us go, please!" Fabiola pleaded.

"Holy Mother!" Martin blurted out; his voice filled with anguish.

Braulio shuddered as he felt a small hand on his left. Turning, he saw her—the little girl from his dreams, the one who had guided him through the corridors. She smiled, and in that moment, Braulio thought it was the most beautiful smile he had ever seen. A profound tenderness filled his heart.

"Is there *kindness* in your heart?" she asked, her voice sweet.

He had heard that question before. Braulio nodded, tears

streaming down his face. The girl smiled tenderly at the hooded figures, who raised their daggers and slashed through the bonds restraining them, except for those binding Agent Estrada, who was slowly regaining consciousness.

"Hey!... What the hell!... Wait... Get me out of here!" he begged; his voice broken.

The others cautiously rose, feeling the numbness in their limbs. The hooded figures remained motionless, and the uniformed man glared at them with hatred. The girl walked to the chapel's entrance and opened the door. Fabiola hugged Braulio tightly, and Martin joined them, the three of them embracing as they walked toward the exit. But the uniformed man blocked their path. He signaled, and two ghostly policemen approached, dragging a box containing the record books.

"What did you plan to do with this?" he asked, gesturing toward the box while menacingly gripping the pointed stick.

The three exchanged uneasy glances, aware that their answer could seal their fate.

"Justice," Braulio replied firmly.

A flash of anger crossed the policeman's face, as if something was gnawing at him from within. In a guttural voice, he ordered, "Get out of here and never return!"

Braulio and Martin hurried to lift the box, carrying it while Fabiola pushed open the heavy wooden door. As they left, they caught a glimpse of the chapel's interior being filled with people of bizarre and macabre appearance. The one who took center stage was the worst of all, his presence malevolent. The chapel door slammed shut behind them. Inside, the officer approached Estrada, who was writhing, trying to free himself.

"Let go of me, you bastard! You don't know who you're messing with. I have strong ties with the cartel," Estrada threatened.

The policeman laughed, a chilling sound.

"Welcome to our circle. If only you could see how much I'll enjoy watching your eyes pop out when I shove this stick up your ass."

A single deranged laugh echoed through the chapel. The last thing Estrada felt was the sharp pain of four daggers plunging into him, his life draining away in a torrent of blood.

CHAPTER 38

Night descended on the hotel as they emerged from the chapel. Despite all logic, they still had their cell phones, which displayed the time: 11:58 p.m. Time had lost meaning during their immersion in the bowels of that cursed place. The stone figure of Saint Francis of Assisi and the Gubbio wolf greeted them, bathed in an eerie luminescence cast by the full moon. Saint Francis's left hand seemed to offer them a blessing, while the wolf appeared meek and friendly.

The apparent calm outside was shattered by a terrifying cry of pain from within the chapel, spurring them into a panicked retreat. Braulio and Martin carried the box, while Fabiola guided them through the darkness.

Their flashlights were gone, but fortunately, the moonlight provided some visibility. They reached the central garden of the hotel, where the contrast between the desolation inside and the beauty and monastic tranquility outside was striking. A shiver ran through them as they heard a bell toll. The sound came from a pole with a small bell hanging from it, and they noticed a human silhouette leaning against it. Their pace quickened.

Just before entering the hotel's main hall, Martin heard a voice call out to him. To Braulio, it sounded familiar. They stopped and set the box down. Martin searched for the source of the voice and saw him standing in a corner beside a beautiful archway decorated with Talavera tiles. It was Martin Robledo, his father. His form was indistinct, but the moonlight enhanced his presence. Tears filled his son's eyes as his father gazed at him with the deep affection only a parent can offer. Martin approached, and Braulio, recognizing the intimacy of the moment, stepped back and embraced Fabiola. Tears welled up in their eyes as well.

The moonlight lent an exceptional tone to the moment as the father apologized to his son for his faults and mistakes.

"I've always carried you in my heart and always will," he said in a loving voice.

Martin forgave him at that moment, and as he did, his father's gaunt face seemed to come to life, resembling the man in the old photographs from his best years. Before his figure faded, he turned to Braulio and said,

"Thank you, *mijo*, for coming to free us."

They grew anxious as they approached the entrance gate, fearing that the security guard on duty—undoubtedly not the same one who had let them in—would identify them as intruders. How could they justify leaving with a box? The guard would likely call the police, and they would be charged with theft. An even greater obstacle loomed: the murder that had just taken place inside the hotel. Agent Estrada was dead. What if they were accused? The investigation could unleash a torrent of misfortune, linking them to the hotel's long history of calamities.

"What do we do?" they wondered, feeling trapped. How were they going to escape?

As they huddled in a corner, weighing their options, they saw someone emerge from the hotel. The figure was carrying what looked like a bundle. They froze, unable to believe what they were seeing. Just when they thought the nightmare was over, a man appeared before them. He was tall, refined, and in his fifties, dressed in an elegant suit, with short, neatly combed hair. His demeanor was sophisticated, and he smiled at them with great kindness.

"Allow me to escort you out, fair lady and gentlemen. Please, follow me," he said politely.

Though skeptical, something about him inspired trust.

They followed him toward a small building. The man opened the door with ease, revealing what appeared to be an abandoned office. With a nod, he beckoned them inside. The room contained a row of dusty desks and chairs. It was dark, but the moonlight filtered through.

They reached a door that opened directly onto the sidewalk along *Niños Héroes Avenue*, as revealed by a nearby window. It must have once been an exit used by the hotel's administrative staff. The elegant man gave the impression that he opened the door with the mere extension of his will. A profound sense of freedom and bliss washed over them as they stepped out. The first thing to touch the external ground was the box—the first step in recovering the condemned memory.

"Wait," he said abruptly. They froze.

"This is for you. I'm confident you'll know how to use it well," he said, gesturing to the bundle he was carrying.

"Be careful; it's quite heavy."

He placed it on the ground.

"I would love to accompany you, but I cannot neglect my duties. I wish you the best that life can offer. Time will tell. *Suum cuique.*" He gave a discreet bow and closed the door behind him.

Just as he had appeared, he vanished into the shadows of the hotel.

The three were stunned. Who was that man? He didn't even give them time to thank him or ask his name.

They inspected the bundle under the street lamps and realized it was a thick black cloth bag, similar to one they had seen before. Braulio knelt and patted it. They exchanged looks of surprise.

He carefully and discreetly unzipped it. A golden glint emerged. Martin quickly ran to retrieve his car from the parking lot and returned within minutes. They placed both treasures in the trunk and sped away from the inn of the condemned, never to return.

CHAPTER 39

Good can emerge from every calamity. Perhaps a cliché, but undeniably true. The events at the *Posada del Sol* left scars on their souls, memories that would haunt them for the rest of their lives. Yet, the ordeal also forged stronger bonds—Braulio and Martin were now like brothers, and Braulio and Fabiola had become engaged, with the date for their union already set. Martin and his wife, Paula, would serve as their godparents.

The large cloth bag brimming with gold centennials brought them significant benefits. They navigated the implications of possessing those coins with intelligence. Accepting ownership was a moral struggle, but ultimately, they reconciled with the idea, convinced that the gold had been given to them with good intentions, reflecting the original benevolence of the hotel. The value lies not in the object itself but in the good it can achieve. Martin's final wishes, as expressed in the video he left for Braulio, were fulfilled.

A great boon reached the hands of Doña Leonor Ortega, the widow of Martin Robledo, ensuring she would live her remaining days free of financial worries.

The most crucial matter, however, was their decision regarding the box's contents and the condemned memory it held. When they arrived at Martin's apartment at dawn, Paula nearly fainted at the sight of her husband's bloodied face and the deplorable state of his companions. The morning sun bore witness to the recounting of that insane tale. Paula, on more than one occasion, nearly went into shock as she absorbed the incredible details, the twists and turns, and their paranormal encounter.

They managed only a couple of hours of sleep, just enough for their minds to organize the ideas necessary to make the right decisions. Several pots of coffee were needed to stay alert. The pervasive corruption within Mexico's police and justice institutions quickly ruled out the idea of handing over the box and filing a complaint. It would only end up buried in a prosecutor's file cabinet after they endured a bureaucratic nightmare. Moreover, such a formal complaint would risk subjecting them to an eventual *"Damnatio memoriae."*

The next day, they debated for hours how to reveal the box's crucial documents and information to the world—a revelation that could shake not only the Mexican State but society as a whole. It could even become international news. They knew powerful entities working behind the scenes would go to great lengths to keep this information hidden. The *Dirty War* in Mexico was far from over; it had simply taken on new names and faces, but its ghostly threat lingered. *Damnatio memoriae* remained a common practice.

CHAPTER 40

The news needed to originate from abroad and be accompanied by viral elements. Martin reached out to a trusted reporter friend who worked for The Washington Post in the United States, sending him everything required for the story. This ensured their complete disassociation from the matter. No investigation would target them, the source would remain fully protected, and antagonistic groups would have little recourse against an American newspaper and journalist. Additionally, the books were digitized and sent via encrypted email and a robust VPN to mask the location, following a suggestion from Martin's reporter friend. After The Washington Post published the scoop, the digital files would be released across all social media platforms and distributed via email blasts.

It took only two weeks to prepare and reveal to the world the journalistic investigation titled, "The Condemnation of Memory in Mexico: A Story of Repression, Terror, and Forced

Disappearance, Now Brought to Light to Deliver Justice to Thousands of the Disappeared and Their Families."

For the occasion, Martin and his family traveled to the city of Chihuahua. They gathered in Braulio's apartment, savoring an exquisite dish Martin had prepared. They toasted to the national news and social networks, which struggled to keep up with the flood of information. Thousands of people were being freed from disgraceful oblivion—justice for the fallen of the *Dirty War*.

THANK YOU FOR MAKING IT THIS FAR!

It has been an honor for me to have you journey through these pages. Now, your voice is essential for this work to continue its life beyond these pages.

I invite you to leave a review and share your thoughts. Your opinion will not only help me grow as an author, but it will also guide other readers who are looking for their next great read.
Leaving a review is simple and can be done on the platform where you purchased this book or on your favorite social media. Don't forget to tag me so I can read your thoughts and thank you personally.

Thank you again for joining me on this literary adventure. I eagerly await your words with anticipation and gratitude.

www.ingramcontent.com/pod-product-compliance
Lightning Source LLC
Chambersburg PA
CBHW030302180626
46810CB00003B/895